Cade

Billionaire Blind Dates

Book 3

Toni Denise

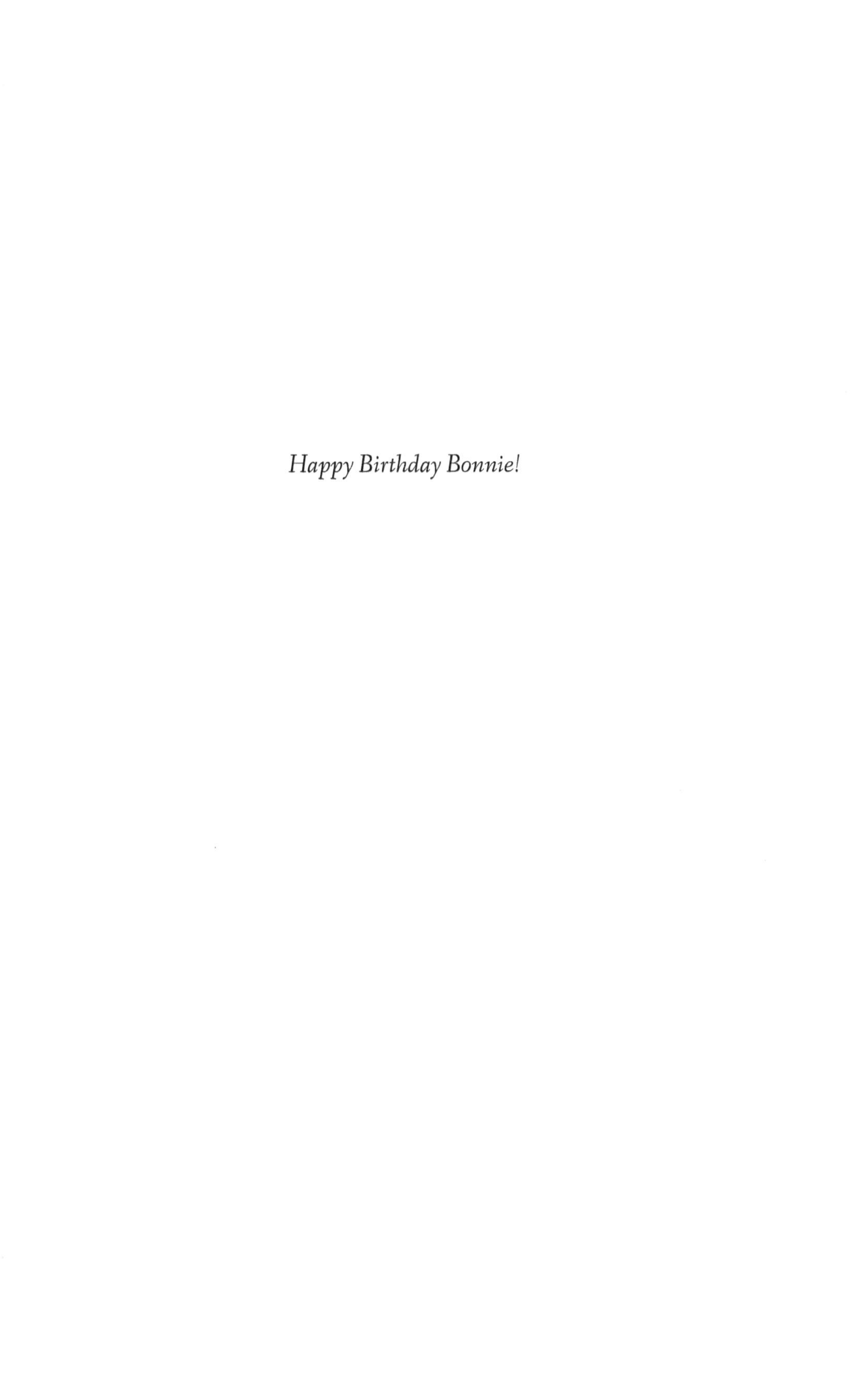

Happy Birthday Bonnie!

Chapter One
Cade

"So, who is next?" Evan laid down his cards and folded.

"It's a little soon for that," Cade said, tossing chips in to raise the bet. He didn't want to talk about dating again just yet.

He and his group of friends met most Friday nights to play poker, and tonight was no exception. However, these games had been more and more rare with the new relationships for three of the six of them.

Almost a year ago now, Evan had come up with an idea to try a blind dating restaurant he was considering investing in. The idea was that the dates were done in the dark, with no info except what you shared, and you couldn't see each other making the success of the date strictly based on your personality.

It was a brilliant concept, especially for their group, considering it was hard to know if women were interested in them or their money and status as successful billionaires. Jake had gone first, and the dates had started off rough, to say the least, and then he'd been set up with Cade's assistant by his sister. It was technically Cade's turn to pick a date for Jake, but Catherine had taken over, and he'd let her.

In the time that all this had been happening, his father had grown increasingly bizarre with his demands of both Cade and Catherine. He'd also taken a personal affront to Jake, dating Lauren, his assistant, and called her some choice names. Cade had done his best to distance himself from his father since then.

Only now, that problem was showing up again. His father had worked with Lauren's mother to almost completely ruin the restaurant. Unfortunately for him, Cade and his friends pulled together to help rebuild it. It left Lauren with a sense of misplaced guilt, with it having been her mother that was involved.

Cade had told no one yet that this latest attack had his father behind it, mostly because he couldn't understand why. Attacking Cade's friends served no benefit that Cade could see and without a motive, he would not solve much. His friends wouldn't be upset with him at all. They'd help him puzzle it all out, but he felt the need to hold this one close.

It pissed Cade off, though. He'd already banned his father from the building of the business he used to run. He had a private investigator looking into him and he'd cross the bridge of what to say to his friends once he knew more. Until then, he'd work to stop his father on his own.

"I think you're up next, Cade," Luke joked.

Cade groaned and ran a hand down his face. "Not if you're picking." Luke had a history of picking the worst dates for everyone.

"I'm offended." Luke pressed a hand to his chest as he pretended he cared. His smile showed how much he didn't care.

"I had to suffer through it. You can pull through," Jake encouraged him.

"Only fair that everyone gets to endure Luke's picks," Evan agreed.

"Help me out here," Cade turned to Ryker. "The longer it takes me to take a turn, the longer it will be before yours."

Ryker remained stoic.

They were an interesting group of guys, Ryker being the quiet one. He only spoke when he felt the need, and those words were usually grunted out. He was Luke's mentor somehow, though. Two more opposite personalities didn't exist.

For every word that Ryker didn't say, Luke did. He was the youngest of the group and his maturity level shined through everything he did in both business and personal life. Luke hadn't matured beyond his teenage years still, despite being several years past them.

Then there were Jake, Evan, and Owen. All three of them had met their significant others on blind dates. Owen hadn't done it at the restaurant like Jake and Evan. It hadn't even been his blind date. He'd accidentally crashed someone else's and ended up with the girl.

"Stop delaying it. You can help us re-open the restaurant." Evan was a not so silent partner with Kayla, the owner of The Blind Date.

He didn't really have a choice unless he wanted to explain why now wasn't a good time in his life to be dating. That was going to happen.

"Fine," Cade grunted out. "He can't go first." Pointing at Luke, Cade leaned back in his chair with a glare.

"You won't know who went first. That's the point." Luke reminded him.

"We all know when it's your turn." Evan rolled his eyes.

Luke grinned, not even bothering to look sheepish about it.

"Deal or not?" Cade asked. He just wanted to move on, back to the game where he could play without too much arguing.

"In the end, Luke is right. You aren't supposed to know who goes first, so can't really agree to it," Jake said.

"Bullshit." He wasn't about to lose this argument. There was no way that he was going to go on his first date in forever with some crazy chick that Luke picked.

"No. You play fair like everyone else did," Evan insisted.

"That's hardly fair. I don't want to do it if I'm just going to go on an awful date with some chick that only wants to sleep with a guy with money." Each of them had more money than they could spend in this lifetime, all of them billionaires. Women were almost always after their money.

"I resent that," Luke said. "Besides, maybe I'm turning over a new leaf."

Cade snorted. "That'll be the day."

"Enough," Owen jumped into the conversation.

"You aren't part of this," Cade reminded him.

"Damn, dude." Owen pushed away from the table and stood. "Anyone want another?"

Cade didn't look around to see who asked for another beer. He tried to focus on the fact that he needed to rein himself in. Mentally, he scolded himself for snapping at Owen.

"We can set you up with that girl from the coffee shop," Evan teased.

"Her name is Paisley. And, no." He had already tried asking her out before everything went sideways in his life. She'd turned him down flat and he had to find a new place to get coffee.

"She's nice," Luke said quietly.

It was such an odd statement from him that everyone stopped and turned. He didn't think women we nice and comment on it. Luke was strictly a one-nighter kind of person and everyone had seen Paisley, knowing she wasn't that at all.

"What?" Luke asked when he noticed everyone looking at him. "She is."

Cade nodded. "She is."

"We're just surprised that you noticed," Ryker pointed out what they were all thinking. "You rarely notice or comment on the ones that aren't willing to bed you right then and there."

Luke crossed his arms and leaned back in his chair, looking every bit the petulant teen despite being 26. "I notice things. This is why I don't say shit."

"No one said anything. We are just surprised." Jake took a sip of his beer, his eyes staying on Luke.

Cade kept his mouth closed as they went back and forth. Taking the attention away from him hadn't been planned, but he'd be grateful and not look this gift horse in the mouth.

"I have feelings, you know," Luke huffed.

Evan bit back a chuckle that turned into a bull blown laugh before he could stifle it. "No one said you didn't."

"You all act like I'm so shallow all the time," Luke complained.

Cade took in the other man's stance and realized something had changed in their dynamic. Luke was no longer relaxed and while his tone was still slightly relaxed, his body was rigid. He stood, flexing his fists as he looked back at his friends.

"Is something going on?" Cade asked.

"No," Luke bit out, too fast.

Cade shrugged. It would come out in time, whatever it was, and Luke would clue them all in when he was ready.

"You can talk to us. Seriously," Owen's laughter had dried up and his tone was more somber.

Luke's eyes cut to Ryker, who gave a small shrug. Then he faced Owen again and shook his head.

"We're here when you're ready." Cade stood and squeezed Luke's shoulder. "We are always here, no matter what it is."

And that was the truth. This group of friends had each other's backs, no questions. Something they all knew about each other, but Cade wasn't ready to put his problems out there yet, either.

Chapter Two
April

April stood, placing her hands on her back and stretching. She'd had her head down at her desk for entirely too long and now she was paying for it. Sore all over, she groaned and added a few twists to her stretching before looking at the clock.

Five hours. It had been five hours since she'd last looked up and taken a breath. April shook her head at herself and bent down to close her laptop. She needed to be in the conference room in less than ten minutes and was wholly unprepared.

It was a wonderful thing that her meeting was with Kayla, a client but also a friend, and she'd spend half their time catching up before they actually got to work. It wouldn't take long for them to make this new contract, anyway.

Kayla was bringing Evan out of the silent portion of their silent partnership officially. It was a simple contract change, one that Kayla didn't need to come in for. April could do it in her sleep. Fact was she could do most of it in her sleep anymore.

She hated her job. Not the clients, except for a few, but she was relegated to doing contracts despite all her years of law school. This wasn't what she intended to do forever and yet it was the only job in law that she'd had. Right after she passed the bar, she was hired here and had worked her way up from lackey to her own clients, but she was bored.

"Keep up the good work," her boss said last night when she left well past dinnertime. "You could be looking at partner before too long."

She shuddered. There was no way she could do contracts for the rest of her life. She'd go insane. Unfortunately, she was too busy to look for a new position and if word got out that she was, she could lose the job she had, which she couldn't afford to do.

No sooner than she sat her laptop down did Kayla walk into the small conference room.

"I brought you something," she sang out, waving a bag of takeout.

Her smile was genuine even as she tried to keep her mouth from watering at the food. Of course, she hadn't eaten since she wasn't watching the time. "Is that for me?" April joked, taking the bag from her friend.

"Tell me you've eaten already today?" Kayla said with concern as she took a seat next to April.

"Lost track of time," April said sheepishly as she dug into the bag. "You didn't?"

April pulled out her sandwich from her favorite café, that wasn't far from her apartment. There was something special about the food there and all of it was amazing and hit the spot every time.

"I figured you hadn't eaten. You're going to waste away, girl." Her friendly tone held an underlying note of sadness and concern.

"I know. I just forget," April told her.

"Set timers. Do something." It wasn't quite a plea, but April knew it was. "I just worry about you."

"I'm fine. Taking a long look at things lately and might be making some changes soon," April confessed.

Kayla arched an eyebrow. "Oh, really?"

"I'm not ready to talk about it yet and it's still just a, maybe."

"Don't leave me without telling me," Kayla teased.

"Afraid you're stuck with me no matter what," April joked back.

The mood sufficiently lightened. They both ate their sandwiches and spoke about the restaurant. It was about to reopen, and April was thrilled for her friend. The restaurant was vandalized and had been closed for a bit. It had been very hard on Kayla to lose the momentum that the restaurant had been enjoying all at once.

It was an interesting concept, but April had never been to the restaurant on a date. She had eaten there but always upstairs in Kayla's office. The novel idea had been turning heads for a while now since Evan, Kayla's boyfriend, had convinced his friends to give it a try. It had leant an air of trust to the restaurant and business had picked up.

Just after the vandalism, April had met all of Evan's friends, only to discover that she already knew one of them, Cade. They'd dated once and Cade's parents had quickly told him they didn't approve of her and Cade had dropped her quickly.

It was a shame because when his family wasn't involved; they got along great. They had chatted about deep, dark things in their life and she had told Cade things that she'd told no one before or since. Cade had seemed open with her as well, but then his father had told him she wasn't a good fit and he'd dropped her so quick.

And he'd dropped her hard. This was the next time she'd seen him, and that was a few years ago. He sent her a text and that had been the last words from him. There'd been no further communication because he'd blocked her. She went to his apartment building once but saw him with another woman, so she'd walked away and assumed that it had all been bullshit for him.

After almost six months of dating, they'd never slept together, a regret. Then, if she had slept with him, she was almost positive that she wouldn't have wanted to stop.

"You good?" Kayla asked.

April shook her head, ridding her mind of the unwanted thoughts. "Sorry. Was zoned out."

"Thinking about anything in particular?"

She shook her head. "Just work, as always."

"Well, I have something to distract you," Kayla grinned.

"Is it more work?" April teased.

"Nope. You're going to try a blind date. I need you to test the new system for me because I trust you, but also because you haven't gone to the old one, so you won't be biased."

April stared at her friend, trying to decide if she was serious. "No way. I don't have time to eat most days, much less to date."

"All the more reason," Kayla pressed. "Please do this for me?"

"No way. I am not letting you manipulate me into one of these dates. I am good right now. Find someone else to be your guinea pig." April stood and carried her trash to the bin while trying to calm herself down.

April knew about the deal between Evan's friends because Kayla had told her. She didn't know who was next, but she was worried enough that it was Cade that she couldn't do this.

"Please, April. I'll be your food alarm forever if you do this," Kayla begged.

"I can't. I really don't have time," April said gently. It was the truth.

"Just one. That's all I ask. Please?" she continued.

"Kayla," April started. "I just can't right now. Plus, I already know it will be one of Evan's friends, so isn't that a lot like cheating?"

"You don't know which one," Kayla pressed.

"I don't want to date a billionaire," April said. "That and there's a one in three chance. I know who it is before I get there. Odds are even better for after I meet them."

"Fine," Kayla sulked. "Let's get this contract done so I can get back to it. You're still going to come by after the kitchen is open again for dinner with me, right?"

"Of course," April smiled. She had no hard feelings for Kayla over her trying to set her up. It wasn't the first time and probably won't be the last one.

They spent the next half an hour adjusting the contract for Kayla to take with her. Perks of knowing your contract lawyer this well was that you got to get your changes done in real time and end your appointment with the finished copy.

"Are you sure I can't convince you?" Kayla asked again as they stood to leave.

"How many times have you tried to set me up?" April asked.

Kayla shrugged, but had to good grace to look sheepish.

"Have I ever said yes?"

"Maybe if you said yes once in a while, I wouldn't ask so much?" Kayla teased.

The women hugged quickly and as they stepped back, Kayla took April's hand. "I just want you to know I am really worried about you. Please take care of yourself better?"

"I'm trying," April promised. "I'll see you later."

She caved. It took an hour after Kayla left for her to give in and text her.

April: Okay, fine. I'll go on your dumb date.

Kayla: Yay!! I'm not even going to ask what changed your mind because I want to capitalize on this before you can change it again.

April: LOL. Well, it probably won't work out, but I'll go 'test things' for you.

Kayla: Nope, not baiting me so you can change your mind again. Putting you in the system now. Download the app.

April: Fine.

She clicked the link that Kayla sent her and downloaded the app to her phone before she could back out. Kayla was right to worry about it.

April: Can you tell me one thing?

Cade

Kayla: Sup?

April: You aren't setting me up with Cade, are you?

Kayla: First, can't tell you. Second, what is your deal with him?

She'd known Kayla since right after Cade had broken things off with her. She'd missed the whirlwind of a relationship that they'd had and had only caught the fallout. Never had she told Kayla who it was and now she really couldn't because they were friends.

Chapter Three
April

One thing she wasn't about to do was ruin some friendships over things that happened in the past that have nothing to do with the other people. Kayla would end her friendship with Cade and it would put Evan in a weird place. As much as she appreciated her friend helping her put herself back together after Cade, this was too personal to share.

April: Nothing.

Kayla: Liar.

Kayla: You're in the system and already have a match. Go get chatting with your mystery man. I bet you'll even like him.

April smiled sadly. That was the entire problem to begin with.

"How's it going?" April's boss stopped by her desk.

"Umm, it's okay. I am actually about to head out, unless you needed something?" she winced at her own people pleasing words.

"Just popping in to check on you. Keeping tabs on those, we are adding to the list of potential partners."

April gave him what she hoped looked like a genuine smile. "Just heading out for drinks with a client," she forced chipper-ness into her voice.

"Amazing," the balding man said, and patted the doorframe before walking away.

As soon as he was out of sight, April blew out her breath. She needed to stop this mess before she ended up as a partner because she didn't want to say no.

Before anyone else could pop into her office, April packed up and headed for the elevator. Once she made it to the ground floor, she'd be home free as long as she didn't answer emails, or phone calls, or text messages.

"Hey," Tucker said as he joined her in the elevator.

Tall, blonde, built, the man was like Thor only here in real life. "Hey," April said quietly. She didn't think she was an overly shy person, but she couldn't form words around him.

"You're leaving early today," he commented.

Her heart lept at the fact that he noticed. "Umm, drinks with clients."

"Ah, knew it was too good to be true. A night where you were free is like a unicorn," Tucker joked.

April forced a laugh, confused.

"How about tomorrow night?" Tucker asked. "I'd love to take you to non-work related drinks if you can swing it?"

April ignored him, assuming he was on the phone or something because there was no way he was talking to her. She wasn't ugly, but she was plain and comfortable with that without issue. No real body issues here despite the drawers of makeup and shapewear she owned. She rarely wore much.

"April?" he asked.

"Sorry?" She stepped to the side, thinking he needed to get out.

"I asked you about drinks tomorrow?"

April bit her lip and looked up at the god of a man. "Me?" she squeaked.

Tucker's smooth chuckle rumbled through the elevator. "Yes. There's no one else in here."

"I thought you were on the phone," she admitted. "I'd love to."

"Awesome. After work, normal work hours anyway?" he asked.

April nodded. "Sure."

The elevator door opened at the ground floor and she stepped out before him. Unsure of what happened to the universe today, April quickly hurried off. She was too far gone to turn back without looking like a fool before she realized she forgot to tell him bye.

She waved down a cab and headed home. In the back of it, she played with the new app on her phone, taking the time to answer a million questions from Kayla's matchmaker settings.

"Here," the driver said.

April looked up, realizing she hadn't even noticed anything about the ride since they left. "Sorry," she muttered.

Paying for the cab, she got out and grabbed her computer bag before closing the door. Her phone was dinging as she walked into her building, and she reached down to flip it to silent. Whoever it was needed to wait. It was probably work anyway.

She spoke to the doorman and headed to her apartment. She didn't have the kind of money for a top-floor apartment, but she did well and didn't mind the apartment she got on the fifth floor. It was almost affordable and spacious by city standards.

Sure, she'd love a view of more than the street, but this was better than she had when she first started working here. One apartment and four women was a cluster that she'd like to never repeat again. There was always drama somewhere between them.

Finally in her apartment, she looked at her phone, noticing that she did indeed have a few work messages. However, there was one message from the Blind Date app waiting for her.

?: Hi. Nice to meet you.

April stared at the message. It was much faster than she expected to hear from someone.

April: Nice to meet you, too.

She set her phone down and went to her kitchen, taking a quick stock of what she had in the fridge. Nothing. Rolling her eyes at herself, she made a bowl of cereal and carried it to the living room, grabbing her phone on the way.

?: Sorry, this is awkward.

April: Agreed.

?: What made you want to do this?

April: Peer pressure.

?: Same.

The conversation was odd. She hated the get to know each other phase of dating. This was even worse because she didn't have work as a safe topic to go back to. Any identifiable information was off limits.

?: What are you hoping for out of this?

April stared at the app. She didn't know what she wanted, probably just that her friend wouldn't ask her to do this again.

April: I'm not sure, to be honest. You?

?: My sister to stop trying to set me up with people, maybe?

April: LOL, same with my friend.

He took his time writing her back, and April thought about who it could be. There were three people left single in Evan's friend's group, and she knew it had to be one of them. Ryker didn't have any family that she was aware of, that and from the things everyone had said, he was into Catherine even if he wouldn't admit it.

While she waited for his response, April switched to a web browser and looked up Luke. Cade definitely had a sister. Though April hadn't met her until recently, he'd talked about her often when they were together. Luke, for all his loud living, was very private about his family, it seemed. She learned he had one sister, younger, but that was it. No information on how much younger or where she lived.

> April: What's another safe topic that isn't banned from the get to know you part of this blind date? Haha.

She relented and sent him a message after he didn't reply while she looked up Luke. With nothing useful to go on, she needed more to know if it was Cade. The one thing she wanted to avoid was Kayla finding out about their past and things getting awkward. She hoped it wasn't him. Luke was a little young, though.

> ?: I don't even know. Favorite food?

> April: Seems safe enough. Confession time, it's going to be weird.

> ?: Can't shock me.

> April: Bet. My go to absolute favorite food would have to be a banana sandwich.

> ?: With cinnamon?

> April: There's no other way.

> ?: I've had one. Can't say it's my favorite, but it's not bad. I had a friend several years ago who liked them.

Cade

April felt her stomach drop. It was Cade, had to be. She had forced him to try one of her sandwiches when they were dating. He'd pretended it was gross and then finished the sandwich off, leaving her without. If it wasn't, she'd be even more shocked.

> April: Cade?

> ?: Dammit.

> April: Seconded. Well, I can tell her I tried.

> ?: April?

> April: Indeed.

She pictured him swearing at his phone on the other end. Probably much more upset by this turn of events than she was.

> April: I'd appreciate it if we kept our past to ourselves, please.

> Cade: Give me your number.

> April: Why?

> Cade: Please.

It wasn't a question, just two demands, one using a pretty word. This was business Cade now, and she knew it. She debated it before sending her phone number over to him and waiting to see what he did with it.

It didn't take long for her to find out. He called and April stared down at the number she didn't recognize, working herself into a full panic. Swallowing it down, she answered,

"Cade?" She was proud that she kept the shakiness out of her voice.

"April," he answered. "I think we need to talk about what's going on and how this happened."

Chapter Four
Cade

Cade pinched the bridge of his nose as he spoke to April. He never thought to talk to her again, and yet, here they were.

"I don't think anyone needs to know that we knew each other once. I agree with you. But I think we need to figure out how to get around this date before we call it off."

"Why?" There was definitely fear in her voice, which made him feel like dirt.

"Because if we just go back and tell them we don't mesh, Kayla will look and see why."

"I don't know what you mean," April said.

"They will look at our chats. Kayla has all the access and I assume she's who set you up with me?"

"I specifically asked her not to let it be one of Evan's friends. I really didn't know." All the confidence in her voice was completely gone, only an apology. He did this to her, and he would never forget it.

"I didn't think you did, April," Cade kept his tone soft. "I'm saying if they look through our chat logs, they will see that we figured each other out and then want to know more."

"Oh," she replied.

"If we don't want them to know about our past, then we need to go on one date and then we can come up with some reason not to go on more." Cade was already thinking about how to get them out of more dates.

"You can tell them I was too dull. It will be believable, and then we can be done after just one."

Cade sighed heavily into the phone as he listened to her meek voice. He didn't want her to be to blame for any of it. She wasn't now, and she wasn't then.

"April," Cade started. "You aren't dull, so it's not believable. We can come up with something, but we don't need to do it tonight."

"I don't think that it's unbelievable, but as long as whatever we say doesn't cause issues between anyone, then I guess it doesn't matter."

"I'm sorry," Cade admitted to her. It was long overdue. "I didn't explain then what happened, and I think I owe you an explanation."

"You really don't," April assured him. "It was a long time ago and nothing we can do to change it."

"I'd like to. I think clearing the air between us might make things easier when we see each other." Cade also just wanted to tell her it wasn't her fault at all.

"Cade, please don't. I'm honestly not sure what I did, but I don't want to hear about it now. It's been a long time and I don't want to figure it out now. I'll leave you alone and try not to be around you aside from this." He heard the quiver in her voice and he broke.

"You did nothing wrong." He told her, needing her to believe him. "I know it sounds so cliché, but I promise it wasn't you, it was me."

April snorted. "Okay."

"My father was going to stop paying for Catherine's school if I didn't cut ties. So I did what he wanted and broke things off to date the person he wanted me to."

"You should have told me," April whispered.

"I was trying to protect her," he told her.

"Always protecting everyone. Who was going to protect you, Cade?" April asked.

Recognizing that it didn't need an answer, Cade continued forward. "So, I broke things off between us and went on to do what he wanted. I never meant for you to think it was your fault or that there was anything you could have done differently. I just wanted to keep you safe."

"What did her threaten you with?" April asked. Her voice was still quiet, but more caring.

"I already told you," he answered.

"No, you said how he threatened your sister, but what did he threaten you with?"

"It doesn't matter," Cade said by way of explanation.

"It does," April insisted.

"We can set the date up soon and then call it good after that," Cade changed the topic.

"Okay."

"Is there a day or time that doesn't work for you?" He needed to get this over with quickly because actually talking to her was bringing back memories that he kept locked away for a reason.

"No. Just after work and I can do any day."

"I'll set it up in the app for as soon as we can, then. I'm really sorry about this, April."

"Me too," April's quiet voice came back again.

Cade ended the call and quickly arranged their date, sending it over to April, and set his phone down. To say his day had taken a turn was an understatement.

In the years since he'd last seen April, he'd managed to push her out of his mind and forget the pain he felt at letting her go. Now, though, the pain was back, and it was worse knowing that she had blamed herself.

He was also completely positive that she had never meant to

reveal that she was taking the blame for the break up. Cade wondered if she even realized what she said.

Either way, now he was going on a date with her again, many years too late. He would take the time to make sure that she knew for sure that she had done nothing wrong with their relationship. He wanted to use the time that they had to spend together to build her back up a little, even if he knew he'd be walking away again.

Talking to her again, hearing her voice, made him realize just how much he missed her. He had told April things that he would never take back, but at the same time he wished had hadn't opened up to her like that. Not because she wasn't a great listener, but because he put the burden of his thoughts on her.

Growing up had been hard with his father. The man wasn't physically abusive, but neither was he kind. Facing the pressure of needing to be perfect and having your whole life planned out before you was stressful.

His father never missed an opportunity to make Cade feel awful or stupid. It was his specialty, always telling him he needed to toughen up and grow a spine. That lasted well into his twenties. Jake was the only other person outside of his mother and sister that knew the true extent of his father's actions.

Cade hadn't given in to his demands much after he'd met Jake and then quickly they had their whole friend group together, something his father had always hated. The words had never stopped from his father. Cade had just gotten better at turning them out.

Then he'd started pressing for Cade to marry. Once that began, it was a whole new level of insults and accusations that questioned everything Cade thought she knew about that man. When that hadn't worked, the insults had moved to Jake and, eventually, Lauren.

To everyone's complete surprise, that was where Cade had drawn the line. While he'd become used to handling his father's special brand of crazy, it wasn't right for him to involve Lauren simply for existing. That had led to Cade cutting him out of his life and the company and to where he was now.

Catherine's voice interrupted his train of thought as she let herself into his apartment. She was always at the highest energy level, and while he loved her, she was a bit too much for him right now. He opened his mouth to tell her so as she sat down next to him.

"I hear you're going on a date?"

How the hell did she know already? "Where'd you hear that one?"

"I know that you're next, so a date must be soon. I wanted to see if I can get in on the pool to throw a woman at you." She winked and slipped off her heels, pulling her feet up on the sofa.

"No." Cade stood, trying to end that conversation.

"I can just ask the guys, but I think I have someone that might be perfect for you," Catherine whined.

"Don't do that voice. It doesn't work on anyone and it sounds terrible," Cade reminded her.

"It works on some people. You're just cold and heartless."

Cade shrugged. He'd been called worse.

"It was worth a shot. But I could make you a deal. If you let me do this, then I won't bother you for a year about dating someone."

A bubble of shocked laughter escaped him. "That's a lie if I ever heard one."

"I'm just trying to be helpful," she smiled back at him.

"You're trying to be a pest."

"I did a good job with Jake and Lauren. Who's to say I wouldn't do that for you, too?"

"I already have a date this week. Let's see how that one goes before we even have this conversation again. What's going on with you?"

Catherine wasn't usually pouty or whiney. She could do it, but normally she was more of the strong, independent type of woman that just demanded everyone follow her lead. It usually worked well for her, too.

"Nothing."

"Now I know you're a liar."

"Mother called. I'm really worried about Father," Catherine bit her lip.

"Do you know where he is?" Cade hadn't been able to locate him anywhere, which was impressive given the number of resources he had at his disposal.

Catherine shook her head. "Mother wouldn't tell me, which is weird, right?"

"Definitely," Cade agreed.

"You know something," Catherine accused him. "I know you do, so tell me."

"I don't know anything." He sighed and gave in. "I think I might know something and when I know for sure, I promise I will tell you. This is too important."

"Or you could ask for help, Cade. I'm not twelve, I actually could be of use."

"I don't doubt it, but it's not good things and I don't want to drag you down in it until I know for certain."

"What kinds of bad things?" There was caution in her voice now.

"Nothing we wouldn't survive. Just keep doing what you do, and I will let you know if there is anything to share soon."

She looked like she wanted to ask more, but stopped. "Fine. Then tell me what you were doing sitting here with the TV off in the half-dark by yourself."

Cade groaned. "Thinking."

"About?" Catherine pressed.

Screw it. He could talk to her because, aside from her name, Catherine knew about April and he'd get to get everything off his chest.

"Do you remember the woman I dated back in college?"

Catherine's eyes got huge. "Is the date with her?"

Cade shook his head. It would defeat the entire purpose of the date if everyone found out. "No. I've just been thinking about her more lately."

"Because you still miss her. And you know that means you should reach out to her again. She should know that she's on your mind. I don't know why you let Father push you away from her anyway."

"You do know why."

"Not everything is your burden to bear alone, Cade. You should have told me and let me see if it was worth it for me."

"He threatened her too." Cade has steel in his voice.

"I know he did, but she might have told you something like you being worth the risk. I've never seen you so light and happy as when you were talking to her, like ever." Catherine rose and came over to him. "I miss Cade, who was a little less stressed about everything."

Cade accepted her hug with a nod. "That won't happen again."

"Be careful Cade, things like that have a way of coming back around and biting us in the ass."

"Even without Father, I don't think she wants anything to do with me, so can't blame her there. Besides, if she didn't meet his requirements then, she definitely wouldn't now, which would only cause more strife."

"Some things are worth it."

"Not me."

Catherine slipped her shoes back on. "I'm heading home. Do something about those thoughts." With that, Catherine let herself out, leaving Cade standing alone with his thoughts in his own apartment.

Chapter Five
April

April sat in the waiting room of the updated and newly reopened Blind Date restaurant, waiting for Cade to show up so they could be seated. She checked her watch again and note that it was already ten past the hours. The Cade she remembered was never late to anything.

"Are you still waiting?" Kayla stopped next to her.

April nodded. Even if she didn't want to have Cade's friends think poorly of him because of her, there was no way out of this one. He wasn't here.

"Maybe he got the time wrong," April offered.

"Unlikely from this person. It'd be more likely that something happened," Kayla, distracted, waved that thought off. "I'll be back in a moment."

April was glad that she wasn't the only one worried about him. She'd been pushing her worry to frustration, reminding herself that Cade had stood her up before with the intention of it being forever. Now that Kayla also seemed concerned, April let herself slip back into worry.

"Ma'am," the host tapped her shoulder. "We're ready to seat you now."

"Oh, umm, okay." She stood and dusted off her skirt.

The man led her back through the dark heavy curtains where another man waited. She knew the concept behind the restaurant, but being here was completely different.

The new man spoke, telling her to put her hand on his shoulder while he led her through the darkness to her seat. It wasn't as dark as she thought it would be, a soft glow illuminated tables which, if you gave your eyes time to adjust, would be enough to navigate.

"Miss, your table is to your right and your date is already seated."

She took her hand off the man's shoulder and slid into a booth's bench. It was weird not to be able to see anything, and she was thirsty, but scared to reach for her cup for fear she'd knock it over.

"I'll be back in a moment with waters and your dishes," the man left them there.

April looked across from her, trying to make out Cade across from her. "Umm, hi," she said.

Cade grunted. "This shouldn't take too long. I think if we stay too long, it won't be as easy for them to believe that we didn't work out."

Taken aback, April had to clear her throat before she could speak. "Sure. Makes sense." She was the fool for thinking they could have any kind of normal conversation. He had suggested nothing like that. She was the fool here for expecting anything else.

Silence hung over her head like a rain cloud, leaving what was already an awkward situation even worse. It was suffocating to sit completely quietly and not even have the body language of the person across from you to go off because you can't see them. Well, she had an outline, but that was barely visible.

Their salads were delivered, and the silence continued. It wasn't until she took her first bite that Cade finally broke the silence.

"Sorry, I was running behind. I had some family stuff to take care of." His words were plain, but his tone showed his anger and frustration.

"With your father?" April asked, not expecting an answer.

"Always," Cade confirmed.

Well, it explained the bad mood even if there was nothing she could do about it. It wasn't like they would be seeing each other again. She was the one that hyped this night up in her head, thinking that they could act normally to each other, like an actual date.

She should have known better than to think anything would ever be different with Cade than the man that had left her. Instead of dwelling on what she'd done wrong, because it had to be something, she pushed her salad around on her glowing plate and waited for the right amount of time to pass before she could leave.

"How is your food?" Cade asked.

April shrugged and immediately felt her face redden. He couldn't see her. "It's okay. I've eaten food from here before, so good as normal. I mean, it's not bad at all. I like the food here. I just don't think I'm hungry tonight."

She rambled when she was nervous. Normally, it was something she could work through to control. However, not with Cade. She barely managed a breath between her words, so of course she'd be looking like an idiot in front of him.

Cade's chuckle had her face on fire. It was bad enough that she knew she'd rambled, but he could have kept his laughter to himself.

"You haven't changed at all," Cade said.

April ducked her head and tried to think of a response to that. That didn't make her sound like more of an idiot.

"It's a good thing," Cade said. "A refreshing reminder of things."

April didn't speak. Cade seemed perfectly capable of carrying this conversation alone.

"I'm sorry for laughing. It's just that you always did that and I had wondered if you still did it. And, well, then you did." There was another chuckle.

"Happy to make your day," April let the bitterness come out in her words.

"April, don't be like that. I'm really not trying to be mean. It was surprising but a good way to know you're still you. I had hoped you didn't change too much."

"That's me. Still awkward as all get out with everyone. Even on pretend dates with people that don't like me. Imagine that." April glanced down at her wrist, only to remember that she no longer wore her smart watch for tonight. That was against the rules. "I'm sure it's been long enough to say it was a bad date and I should be able to go."

"Wait. We haven't even decided what to tell her."

"Tell who? Kayla?"

There was a pause from Cade followed by a quiet, "yes."

"I told you. Just tell her I was boring as hell. It's believable and gets her off my back for a while and then you can return to your regularly scheduled programming with dates that might putout for a change. I've got to get going."

"You can't," Cade stopped her.

"Yes, I can." April made to get up and Cade pressed a button on the table, turning the light from a soft green to a bright red.

"You just need to wait for someone to come to walk you out. I called them over."

"Thanks," April muttered. This date couldn't get much worse. "Tell Kayla whatever you want. I'll go along with whatever."

"I didn't mean for this to be a shitty night, April," Cade told her.

"You never mean anything," April bit out, standing as the server returned to the table.

It was no problem leaving the restaurant, as her eyes were now very accustomed to the soft glow. It was like a weird maze that you couldn't touch the sides of. She managed to make it out without making a terrible mess of anyone's dinner, though.

She did not need to speak to Kayla. Cade to say whatever he wanted and just go along with it later. April needed to get out of here, and as quickly as possible, before she managed to embarrass herself with the lights on, too.

April scanned every passing car as she rode in the back of the taxi, half expecting Cade to be right beside her at any stoplight, waiting for her to mess up again. It would just complete her night to embarrass herself again for him.

She probably should have stayed and powered through instead of letting him see how much his words affected her. There was no way she could have, even in the dark, though.

When she made it to her building and hadn't seen Cade again, April breathed a sigh of relief. At least her embarrassment was over for now, maybe forever, with Cade. She'd just have to keep turning down invitations from Kayla where Cade might be.

Her phone rang and April debated not answering. It was Kayla, and she'd asked her to come up and see her after the date and she obviously hadn't. Unsure if she would show up out of concern, April answered it.

"Hey, sorry. I just got home," April answered.

"I'm sorry he was such a jerk. He told me he was some family mess going on and while it's no excuse, I just wanted to assure you that I would never set you up with an asshole," Kayla explained.

April let out a sad laugh. "I know you wouldn't. It's okay though, not going to get it perfect every single time. Sometimes people just aren't a match."

"I was so sure, though. You guys seemed perfect."

"Kayla, it's okay. I am going to shower and crawl in the bed. I'll talk to you tomorrow about it and how the restaurant experience was."

"Thank you. I'm so sorry."

April got off the phone and shook her head at herself. She should not get butterflies at the fact that Cade hadn't told Kayla anything to make April look bad. That was common courtesy of telling the truth. Instead, her stomach did flips. She was an idiot.

Chapter Six
Cade

Cade sat by the pool, looking out over the waterfall feature he'd had installed. He didn't swim much, but the sound of the water was relaxing and the whole setup was unlike anything you'd find in the city. It was something he insisted on, making the feature unique but realistic, if not out of place.

He loved living in the city and the convenience that came with living there, but one of the first big purchases he made was this house outside of the city in the suburbs, just for him to retreat to, away from everyone and everything.

His friends visited often, and he used to host parties out here that would last an entire weekend, but he hadn't done that since a client tried to force Lauren into something she wasn't interested in. It had been an absolutely awful thing to see her scared like that. Since then, it was close friends only.

If anyone so much as thought about doing that to April, he'd... well, he'd do nothing because she wasn't his. Even if he was thinking about changing his mind about her, he ruined any chance of that on their fake date.

His mother had chosen his drive over to call him, and that had set him in a particularly foul mood. There was no getting out of the date that late and he couldn't calm his anger, so even though he didn't mean it, April took the brunt of his emotions.

Cade wished things were like they had been with her. If they were, he would have told her everything and she would have found some way to soothe him or put it into perspective. Hell, she probably would have found a way to make him laugh.

Damn, he missed her. He'd never admit it out loud, but he missed her since he pushed her away the first time. It was worse now that she was actually just a phone call away. Somehow, the date only made it worse because he didn't get to see her. He probably would have caved, though, if he would have seen her face crumple when he hurt her feelings.

Kayla hadn't let up on him either, wanting to know what happened. It meant that April hadn't said anything about the way he treated her, which was weird. He expected her to tell Kayla what an ass he was.

Instead, he'd told on himself that he was in a bad mood before the date started and had been rude. Kayla was understanding, knowing that there was family drama behind things and that was the reason he was late, but now she wanted to know exactly what he'd done and why he wasn't willing to fix things.

He laughed and shook his head at himself. There was no fixing anything between them. He'd made sure of that more than once.

Cade tossed back the rest of his beer as his phone rang. The caller was a number he didn't recognize, and he hesitated to answer. He didn't want to work this weekend, and it was likely a client.

On a sigh, he answered it anyway. "Cade," he said to the caller.

"I know damn good and well who I called. What a shitty way to answer the phone," his father's voice boomed through the phone.

Stunned, Cade took a moment to gather his thoughts, ignoring his snide comment about how he answered the phone. "Father."

"Yes, amazingly, I know who I am, too."

He had a thousand questions going through his mind. Cade

needed to know what he wanted from him and his friends and why he was doing the things he was doing. He also wanted to keep him on the phone long enough to send a message to Ryker's tech guy and have him trace the call.

"What do you want?" Cade asked. Sticking with his normal brusque demeanor, he tried not to let his father know that he was eager to talk to him.

"I want you to stop playing these games," his father shouted.

Cade was mid-text and paused, confused. "What games?" He wasn't the one playing them, his father was. He finished the text and sent it off, hoping the man was paying attention and would trace the call.

"I know you were at that restaurant to meet a stranger," he bit out.

"First, I didn't hide that I was going, so I'm not even going to bother asking you how you know. Second, my dating life is none of your business." Of all the places this conversation might have gone, this was definitely nothing he would have guessed.

"I raised you better than to be out there dating random people in the dark, doing who knows what in the dark, and probably setting yourself up with a gold digger like your secretary. Hell, it might even be her. Maybe she lets you and Jake share."

Cade clenched his fists and stood. He was in need of a punching bag before he used a wall instead. "Don't talk about her like that. You don't even know the woman, and she's not with anyone but Jake."

"I guess he's got plenty of money for her for now. I'm sure she'll be hitting on you again before too long."

"What the fuck is your problem?" Cade demanded.

"My problem is my son is out there acting a fool. You let one of your best clients go over that woman!" He was yelling now and Cade could picture his round face as red as a cherry by now.

"He tried to hurt her!" Cade shouted back. He forced himself to unclench his fist and take a deep breath.

"She asked for it and you need to wise up before some little whore comes and takes all my money."

"It's my money now. You are no longer a part of the company."

"Semantics. I made that money. You wouldn't be where you are if it weren't for me," his father chuckled. "I bet it eats you up, knowing that you are living off of my hard work."

"What do you want?" Cade said through gritted teeth.

"I want you to get serious. You need to get married and make sure this company stays in the family. It's past time for you to start training a son of your own."

"What year do you think it is? I don't need an heir and a spare. We aren't royalty." He'd roll his eyes if he wasn't so confused by all of this.

"Might as well be royalty when it comes to business. Your time is running short to make an advantageous marriage, Cade. Move the company forward and do what you know needs to be done."

"I have no desire to make an advantageous marriage and you have no right to tell me what to do." His jaw ticked as he tried to keep his anger under control.

"Quit playing your games because you're made at me and do what you know is the right thing here."

"The right thing for me to do would be to end the call and not have to deal with your shit any longer. However, I'm still here for now."

"Bad things happen to people that don't follow the rules, Cade," he threatened.

Oh, that got his attention more than anything else.

"Like fights on the street? Vandalism? Anything else?" Cade tipped his hand.

There was a pause as Cade imagined his father sorting out the facts that Cade must already know.

"I know about Lauren's mother. If you think of trying anything like that again, I promise you I won't bother trying to hide anything from anyone, and I'll let you go down for your crimes like anyone else would." Cade felt empowered for the first time in weeks when it came to his father.

"I dare you to try it. You have no proof of anything, and there's nothing connecting me to whatever you're talking about."

Cade smiled. "That's where you're wrong. I know all about Lauren's mother and the deals you made with her. She's keeping her mouth shut for now, but I can only imagine how a little money might tip things in my favor. Or I could do one better and release the emails you sent her, complete with IP addresses. Here's a tip for you. Next time, don't use your fucking home computer to set up crimes," Cade snapped.

Not waiting for a response, Cade ended the call and gripped his phone, barely holding back from tossing it across the yard, maybe into the in-ground pool.

The man had lost his mind. There was no other excuse for what was happening. A wife? An heir? Who the fuck demands their kid get married to carry on the legacy of their business anymore? He had so many questions.

With no one to vent to about it, Cade set his phone on the pool chair and went inside. He wasn't answering it again this week, and he needed a fight.

Pausing for only a moment as he entered his home gym, Cade took a steadying breath and let loose on the heavy bag in front of him.

Chapter Seven
April

It was Monday night, and April was still at work, well past dinnertime. She hadn't realized it until someone pointed it out, as usual. It wasn't even that she enjoyed this job. She was just hyper-focused on everything she did. It was a bad habit when you didn't have someone reminding you to take a break.

It was almost easier for her to work a dead-end job because people told her to take breaks. Here, they encouraged you not to. Wanted to eat? Then you should be taking a client out for dinner.

She arched her back again. The standard end of the day, work out the kinks she'd put there during the day movement that had become her routine.

A buzzing called her attention and April shuffled around the piles of paper on her desk, looking for her phone. It was on vibrate and loud enough to have other people looking over at her as it continued to rattle on the desk.

"How's it going, April?" Mark, her boss, stopped by her desk.

"Just looking for my phone," she told him, still trying to find the source of the noise.

He laughed, his too loud, annoying as anything laugh, and

reached down on her desk, picking up her phone. "You'll be partner before too long with this kind of dedication. No one wants to separate themselves from their phones anymore and you can never find yours." He laughed again, his toupee in danger of falling off if he threw his head back any further at his own joke.

She took her phone and seriously considered looking for a cleaning wipe before using it. "Thanks. I'm about to head out for the night," she told him.

"Really? I'm surprised at you leaving while others are still here. You're usually last." He sounded disappointed in her, and April had to remind herself that she didn't care.

"I have dinner plans," still making up her excuse, she tried to tidy her desk before leaving.

"Just the same, we prefer your full dedication," he winked like it was a secret.

She didn't gag, despite his best efforts at making her come close. He wasn't hitting on her, so there was that. It was just that he really thought she wanted to work like this forever and she really didn't.

"Understood," April replied and gathered her purse, slipping past him. "I've really got to get going."

"You aren't going to take your computer?" He sounded shocked.

"I'll be back here early in the morning, as always. At some point, I've got to get some rest." She made her way to the elevator and pressed the down button, waiting for the doors to open as Mark followed.

"It's a shame we have to sleep. It'd be so nice if those of us that were dedicated to our jobs would be able to get even more done. It's definitely why we're single, right?" He grinned again.

April shuddered but was saved from replying by the ding of the elevator arriving. "Have a good night," she said as the doors closed behind her.

Did people really think she was dedicated to her job instead of dating? She wasn't, intentionally. At some point, she'd just given up on trying to date and work had filled her time.

Shit, he was right. This wasn't what she wanted for herself. It was the farthest thing it could be from what she'd imagined her life would be now.

The saddest part was that it was Cade that had sent her down this path. At one point, all her future dreams had included Cade, and she'd just never bothered to come up with new ones when he left.

It wasn't lost on her how lame that sounded. As she stepped out onto the ground floor, she checked her phone, wondering who was calling her earlier. Kayla was her only missed call and April pressed send on her contact as she climbed into the back of a cab.

Driving around the city wasn't worth the headache of parking, so she'd sold her car several years ago, opting to have someone else drop her off.

"You're still at work, aren't you?" Kayla said as she answered the phone.

"I'm not," April defended herself.

"I hear traffic. You just left, didn't you?" Kayla asked.

"Maybe," April answered sheepishly.

"I'd fuss at you, but I don't think it's doing any good. I called for another thing, though,"

"Oh?" April waited for her friend to get to the point.

"I want to know what happened with your date. And before you give me anymore of that nonsense, I want the actual truth. I know it was something more than you've been telling me because neither of you will talk about it or give it a second try."

"Kayla—"

"No," she interrupted. "Business aside, I want to be your friend again, April. We never get to talk anymore and I know something is going on. I just wish you'd talk to me." Kayla's sad voice was quieter than usual. "I miss you."

April missed her, too. She wanted to talk to someone about all the things that were going on in her life and have them listen and give a damn.

"Drinks?" April asked.

"Working," Kayla answered.

"Ironic," April couldn't help pointing out.

"Come here. I'll order some food and you can talk to me," Kayla offered.

"You're working. I don't want to interrupt."

"I'm the owner. I can do what I want. Come on by. I'll order food now and see you soon." Kayla ended the call before April could argue again.

She needed her friend, and it was time to let her in. April leaned forward and gave the driver updated directions. Leaning back, she let herself smile as she thought about finally letting someone in.

It was a quick trip to the restaurant, much closer than her house. Walking in, she avoided everyone's gaze as she slipped past them and headed for the stairs that led to Kayla's office.

"I should have figured you just left work. I thought you'd be a little longer," Kayla greeted her as she entered her office. "The food is on its way and it's not salad."

"I would have just eaten salad. Let me know what I owe you." April reached into her purse for her wallet.

"First, absolutely not just a salad. I got meals and desserts. I don't know what's been going on, but we have a lot to catch up on. And second, why would I ask for money from you? I swear it's like my friend completely disappeared."

April offered a sad smile and dropped into a chair. "She might have."

Kayla took the seat next to her. "Oh, honey. What's wrong?"

"I hate my job. I hate it so much. I'm good at it. I never leave, but I don't want to do it. They keep talking about partner options and I don't want it. I don't know how to say I don't want it anymore without losing my job and I just want to quit, but I can't afford it." April rushed it all out.

Kayla stayed quiet, knowing her friend well enough to know she wasn't done yet.

"And the date. It was all fake. I figured it out the first night and we decided to follow through with the date so you wouldn't know."

"You know Cade?" Kayla asked.

She nodded. "Remember when we met, and I was going through that nasty breakup?" April waited for her friend to put the pieces together.

"That asshole was not Cade. There's no way."

"I promise you it was. It wasn't until we all met at Catherine's that I saw him again. He disappeared really good and then all this time goes by and suddenly he's there again."

Kayla pulled her into a side hug. "I'm so sorry. I never would have set you two up if I had known. I thought with the way that Cade was watching you that he was into you. And you never need to hide anything from me, ever."

"I know. I just didn't want to be the cause of any friction between friends. It didn't seem right, especially as it was so long ago. It's not even important enough to worry about, so please don't tell anyone."

"No. You're important. Your feelings are important and don't you let anyone tell you any different."

April smiled at her friend.

"Food," a man called from the top of the stairs.

"Oh!" Kayla jumped up. "I'm so glad I ordered dessert now." She ran to meet him and grabbed the bags before bringing it back to her office.

The scent of grease hit her in the face. She never ordered fries anywhere anymore. It was too easy to eat too many. Tonight, she wanted them all.

"Tell me what happened on the date," Kayla said as she pulled the food out.

As they unwrapped their burgers, April explained it all. The lie, the rudeness, her misinterpretation of everything. By the time the fries were gone, April had shed more tears than she had in years and felt equal parts completely drained and re-energized.

"Thank you for coming," Kayla said as April made to leave.

"Thank you for making me. I needed this."

They hugged again, and April headed out to the waiting car that Kayla had called for her. She wasn't sure what happened next, but she knew she felt like the weight of her thoughts was getting lighter for now.

She decided to do one last thing before she made it home. It was only fair that Cade knew that Kayla was aware that they knew each other now. She sent a quick message and silenced her phone, not caring if he wrote her back.

April: I told Kayla everything about us. Sorry.

Chapter Eight
Cade

Cade picked up his phone again, looking at the message from April. He hadn't opened it yet and couldn't preview the entire thing. It had been there since last night and he still couldn't decide if he wanted to know what she had to say.

Before she messaged him, he had convinced himself that he was never going to hear from her again, even if it meant one of them avoiding all mutual social situations. Whatever she wanted now probably wasn't good news. The side eye that Lauren gave him this morning pretty much confirmed it.

"Lauren?" Cade hit the mic on his desk.

"Yes, Cade," Lauren replied.

"Did my next meeting cancel?" Cade checked the clock. It was already five minutes past.

"I would have told you if I had that information," she said, annoyed.

"Thanks. Just checking." He let go of the mic and leaned back in his chair. He needed to see what April had said so he could start his own damage control.

Cade swore and grabbed his phone again, just as it started to ring.

Half expecting it to be her, he looked at the unknown number and knew it wasn't. It was his father again.

He declined the call and unlocked his phone, going to his messages to read hers. Before he could read it, the phone rang again from the same unknown number.

"What?" Cade said, answering the call and putting the phone to his ear.

"I've already told you about answering the phone like that," his father's scolding voice came through the speaker.

Cade bit back a swear and gripped the phone tighter. "I've also told you to leave me alone."

"I will not. You are my son and, like it or not, you have responsibilities to live up to. One of them means getting married and carrying on the family legacy."

"What the fuck is wrong with you?" Cade ground out. "This isn't the dark ages and things don't work like that. I don't need to get married or produce an heir and a spare."

"Just because you refuse to accept it doesn't make it less true," his tone had gotten calmer.

Cade sighed. "I'm not doing with you. I am not getting married until if and when I want to. Leave me and my friends alone."

"If you want me to leave them alone, then you need to do what I want," he replied, his tone even and calculated.

He'd walked right into that one. "Ah, so you admit that you are behind all of this?" Cade asked, trying his best to sound nonchalant.

"I've done nothing of the sort. Now, Amanda is a brilliant choice in a wife and I will send you her contact details."

Cade's mind hatched a plan, and the words were out before he could overthink things. "All you want is for me to get married?" he asked.

"Almost. You need to bed her fully and produce an heir," his father said matter-of-factly.

"I can't guarantee how long that will take. Is the marriage enough to get you to leave all of us alone, me and my friends, their partners, and my sister?"

"You let me worry about your sister," his father pushed back. "The rest, yes, for now."

"Fine," he gritted his teeth even as he agreed to the nonsense.

"Good. It's about time you showed some good sense. I'll send Amanda's contact information over and she will be waiting for your call."

Cade didn't argue. He had absolutely no intention of contacting her, but his father could believe whatever made him happy.

The call ended and sure enough, a contact was sent via message shortly after. Cade opened it so it would show read, but then closed it back out.

He went over his plan in his mind a few times before returning his thoughts to work. Ignoring April's message for the moment, he finished out his next meeting. The message notification teased him as he tried to ignore it for now.

It was a damn good thing that his client was late as it was because Cade had also been late to the meeting and was completely distracted. His plan would work. It had to. He tossed the ideas around in his head as the other man talked business and looked for flaws in it.

He was playing a dangerous game, and he knew it, but there was little he could find to fault the plan. Now, to convince the other person might be a little more difficult.

One more meeting to get through and he'd be free from work obligations for the night. Taking the chance now, he read April's message.

Cade let out a loud laugh as he read it. She'd told Kayla that they knew each other. It was almost too good. Everyone would be slightly less surprised by what he was about to ask her then.

He sent off a quick message to her before his next meeting showed up.

Cade: Meet me tonight.

No sooner than it sent, bubbles appeared from April. He didn't get to see the response as Lauren interrupted to let him know his last meeting was here.

"Send him in," Cade replied, setting his phone face down and getting down to business.

The meeting ran longer than expected, partly due to the fact that Cade wasn't focused. He had to remind himself more than once to take his eyes off his phone. This was an important contract he needed to stay on top of.

"Cade, is there something going on?" the older man across from him finally asked.

Taking a deep breath, Cade decided it was now or never. "Actually, you can be the first to congratulate me on my impending nuptials." He pushed a smile across his face.

The man stood and took Cade's hand, giving it a firm shake. "Congratulations, son. I know you'll make some lady very happy."

"I hope to, sir," Cade replied.

"You should have rescheduled this meeting. When is the big day?" the man started towards the door.

"I'm trying to set it as soon as possible. We don't want anything big or showy." Well, he didn't, anyway.

"That's a sign of a good woman when they don't need to show you off. Happiness is about so much more than other people's opinions on your relationship." He grabbed the door handle. "Let me know when you're back to work after the happy day. We can meet then. You might be less distracted," he laughed at his own words. "Or more. Time will tell."

Cade walked to the door with him and saw the man out before telling Lauren she could take off for the day. She looked at him questioningly, but didn't voice any of her thoughts.

He waited until Lauren left before closing the door to his office and picking up his phone to see if April had written him back. It was well into dinnertime now and he'd take her out somewhere nice if she was willing.

> April: You can come by my place. I'm tired
> and not in the mood to fake nice to other
> people tonight.

Cade snorted. If she only knew what he was about to ask her, she'd probably prefer the public instead.

> Cade: I'll bring dinner so you don't have to
> cook. What's the address?

He knew it already, but there was no reason she needed to know that.

> April: I'm already cooking. Feel free to stop
> by and I'll feed you too.

She sent her address and Cade didn't fight the genuine smile that was creeping across his lips. April was surprisingly agreeable tonight, and he could only hope that the trend continued.

Cade told her he was on his way and quickly headed out. He had a feeling time was of the essence, and he needed to get to her before she changed her mind.

Chapter Nine
April

April stood in her kitchen cooking dinner and obsessively checking her phone. She kept waiting for Cade to change his mind and say he wasn't coming, but he hadn't.

Honestly, she'd invited him over to her place, expecting him to say no. Now she was cooking dinner for two and still dressed after a long day at work, when she wanted nothing more than to slide into comfy pajamas. The cooking she'd be doing either way, but with fewer ingredients.

He kept surprising her, just not in good ways. Now she was terrified of what he wanted if he was willing to come over to have the conversation. Then again, the man was something to look at it.

No. She shook her head. She did not need to go there at all, she reminded herself. Cade was trouble, and it always ended that way. No matter how her body responded to him, she needed to hold her resolve.

Curiosity was definitely getting the better of her. She should have told him no when he asked to meet. She absolutely shouldn't have invited him to her place.

It was a cycle she'd been stuck in since she sent her address to him. One minute she was lusting after him, the next she was sick to her stomach with worry over what he wanted.

April pulled the garlic bread out of the oven and set it on the stove to cool. Her shrimp Alfredo was just finishing, and now all she needed was for Cade to show up so they could eat. Or she could start without him just to show that she wasn't waiting for him.

Before she could fix her own plate and congratulate herself for that thought, her intercom buzzed with Cade's voice. Her palms immediately started sweating and she wiped them on her skirt before she pressed the button to let him up.

It wouldn't take him long. She was only on the second floor, no view, but it was cheaper that way. April rushed to the mirror by the door and took a second to fix her hair before he knocked. She didn't want to look like she was trying, but she wasn't going to be a mess, either.

Her heart lept into her throat as he knocked and she had to swallow the lump back down. There was no need to be nervous, she reminded herself as she opened the door.

Cade stood there in his tailored suit looking every inch the businessman. She knew he would be fit under that jacket, not that she'd seen him without one in years, but she just knew. Before her mouth could start watering, she moved out of his way and let him in.

"Thanks for having me over," he said as he walked past her.

Him standing there, looking like a giant in her small living/dining area, made her feel like shit. She shouldn't, but she couldn't help but notice that she didn't measure up to him.

"Sure. Let me get plates and we can take them to the sofa." April pointed at the sofa, as though he needed help to find it, and then shook her head at herself.

He made himself comfortable as she put dinner together. It didn't take long and she carried two plates to the coffee table. "Can I get you wine or water?"

Cade cleared his throat, "water, please."

She nodded and went to the kitchen, coming back with a bottle for each of them. "Bottled okay?" internally, she groaned. It wasn't like she had another option unless he wanted tap.

"Thanks," Cade took the bottle from her.

April took an awkward seat next to him. As they ate in silence, she cut her eyes to him and noticed that he wasn't relaxing. He sat on the edge of the sofa, holding his plate.

"Sorry," she said after finishing her next bite. "We probably should have gone somewhere instead. I was just really tired and not wanting to go out."

"This is fine. The food is really good." He said it, but he still looked incredibly out of place.

"Thanks," she mumbled.

It was like he had looked around her place and judged it, finding her wanting. Taking her plate to the kitchen, she took a moment to gather her strength before facing him again.

"Where do you want these?" Cade's voice came from directly behind her.

"Oh," she squeaked. "Umm, just in the sink is fine. I'll do the dishes later."

He nodded. "You made dinner?" he asked as he looked around.

April nodded. "Yeah. Can't afford to eat out all the time, so I learned to make what I liked." In college, she'd been frugal, but she still wasn't much of a cook.

"You learned well. No surprise there. You were always good at anything you put your mind to."

Was that a compliment?

"It was a compliment," Cade laughed.

Shit, that was supposed to be an inside thought. "Uh, thank you?"

"You're welcome. I meant it."

April nodded and tried to catch her breath as Cade overtook the space. He wasn't doing anything but existing, but he filled the room with power regardless.

"What did you want to talk about?" she asked.

"A few things, actually. Should we go back to the living room?"

April followed him, but as he took a seat on the sofa, she sat on the floor across from him with the coffee table between them.

Cade arched an eyebrow at her, but didn't comment on her choice of seating. She needed distance.

"I wanted to ask you for a favor. It's a big one, but I will make it fair to you."

It was her turn to arch a brow at him. Her mind was blank as she tried to figure out what Cade would want from her, of all people.

"If you agree, I will explain the reasoning, but I'd rather not without your agreement because of the personal nature of it. Then we'd need an NDA and a contract, but I trust you to make the contract."

More confused, April shifted on the floor and pulled her feet under her. He had her attention. She'd give him that much.

"I'll be honest, Cade. I can't think of a single thing I could help you with. You have lawyers that can write your contracts, so it's not that unless it's something clandestine, which I'll save you the trouble and tell you no now."

Cade coughed to cover another laugh. "You are somehow both very wrong and very close."

Frustrated, April blew out a breath and ran a hand through her hair, shifting her part. "Just get on with it."

"I want you to marry me."

Her mouth fell open, and she had no power to close it. Never in a million years could she have guessed that. "I'm sorry. What?" Not that long ago, she wanted him to ask. Now? Now she was just confused, even as her heart shouted yes.

"It only needs to be for a few years and it would not be in name only. I need children."

April tilted her head as she studied him. "Are you sick?"

"No."

"I have questions," she said before she stood. "I also need a drink."

"Got anything stronger than wine?" Cade asked.

"No," April said but poured two glasses. Grateful that he didn't follow her, she took several deep breaths to get her thoughts in order. "Here," she said, handing him a very full glass.

"I expected you to have questions, April."

Her head whipped up. Him saying her name had some weird effect on her. "Why me?"

It was Cade's turn to tilt his head. "Not what I expected you to go with first."

It wasn't what she meant to say first either, but here they were.

"We know each other, and I already know that our personalities are compatible. It would work," he explained.

"We don't know anything about each other. It's been years."

"People don't change that much," he told her.

"They do. They do it all the time. I thought I knew you and then one day you were gone. I never would have thought the Cade I knew would have done that, but he did. Maybe it's just me that doesn't know you, then."

Cade studied her. "I would like to explain. I can't until you agree."

"Cade, I know it was your family. I'm more concerned that you walked away from me like that. Why in the world would I want to marry someone who can just leave at the drop of a hat?" April paced across the small living room. "I have nothing to offer here. No money. I know you can find women a lot prettier. No power. I don't get it and you're going to have to explain."

"April," Cade started.

"No." She held up her hand. "I wasn't fishing for a compliment there. I'm not a knockout, but I'm not ugly. I'm comfortable with who I am," most of the time.

"It would be a contract marriage. You can draw it up and we will agree on our terms and custody up front. I need this, April, or I wouldn't be asking."

"No. That's not good enough."

"Fine. But please stop pacing. It's driving me nuts." April tossed him a look that said she didn't care. "I need your word that you won't say anything to anyone about this. No matter what you answer."

"You didn't bring an NDA with you?" April asked, honestly shocked.

"No. No one knows I'm here. I trust you to agree not to tell anyone, and I am still hoping that you'll say yes."

"You have my word. None of this conversation leaves this bubble right now." She agreed. They'd often had talks that were extremely private and had stayed in their bubble, as they called it.

"Thank you. My father is behind all the damage to the restaurant and a few other things that you probably don't know about."

She was losing count of the times he had shocked her tonight. "Okay?"

"He is demanding me get married and have him grandchildren, and he will stop. It makes as much sense to me as it does to you. I have people looking for him, but right now, the best way to stop the damage is to give him what he wants."

April did stop pacing as her brain started the mental gymnastics it needed to do to make this make sense. "Your friends don't know?" she asked.

Cade shook his head. "They don't, and I don't want them to."

She stopped pushing her feelings down and let herself feel bad for him. "You know they won't think worse of you, right? I've met all your friends, and they are great. They would support you."

"I don't want them involved in this. Besides, I can't find him anywhere to do anything about it, and he's just sending others to do the damage for him."

"What exactly does he want from you and, by extension, me?"

"For me to carry on the family name and create an heir."

"You could do that with a surrogate," April argued.

"If you don't want to make this marriage that real, we could do that. Or even IVF."

"That's not what I meant."

"I know. I can also make you look much more desirable for the partnership in your firm. I have power and influence, and you would, by extension."

Ironic that what he was offering was so far off from what she wanted. "I need one thing from you before we can talk, Cade. Why did you leave before, and what would I have to say that it wouldn't happen again?" She waited for his answer, needing to know what it was.

Cade sighed. "I can't answer that one without your agreement on this."

April put her hands on her hips and stared him down. "That doesn't make any sense. Whatever it was that I did to upset you back then can hardly just be talked about after I agree to marry and sleep with you."

"April—" Cade started, but she cut him off.

"No. I'm done." Shaking her head at herself, she tried to make sense of the last few minutes and what had happened to her rational brain just because Cade was the one with this insane offer. "I can't believe that I was even entertaining this thought. Why would I? So I could be in custody court with you later on when I do something else to piss you off? Get out, Cade."

April pointed at the door. Cade looked like he wanted to say something, but wisely kept his mouth shut and let himself out.

She sunk down onto her sofa after locking the door. There was no reason for her to entertain that offer. It was bizarre, and she was better than that. It was better than tying her life to a man who so clearly didn't want her and ending up stuck in a one-sided marriage for who knows how long.

It wasn't Cade she was mad at. It was her for nearly giving in to what he wanted, despite her own needs. She needed to do better at shielding herself around him or work better to not be around him. Anything was better than the way she felt right now, angry at herself, embarrassed, and alone.

Chapter Ten
Cade

"Y ou know that Lauren is my employee, right? Like she has actual work to do?" Cade asked his sister, Catherine, as she took a seat in his office.

"You know that I don't buy that tough guy act, right?" Catherine waved him off. "Besides, this time, you invited me here."

"To talk to me. Not to stand out there and talk to Lauren for half an hour," Cade persisted.

"Whatever. You have no issues with how she does her job. We both know all this is nonsense, and I'm not even sure why you bother with it." Always one to call him out, Catherine didn't wait for him to acknowledge that he was right. "Now, I have been up here too long already, so if you wouldn't mind getting to the point."

He had no issues with Lauren's job. She was right on that front. It was more of a habit now to tease the two women about being friends whenever Catherine visited his office. Lauren would never let her job slip in favor of chatting.

It also gave him a bit of a buffer right now because he needed to be delicate about what he wanted to ask her. He hoped she had a clue where their parents were, and if he could just get a line on him, he might figure out what his next move would be.

"Do you know where mother and father are?" Cade asked directly.

Catherine shook her head. "Mother calls here and there, but never from the same number, if it even shows up on my phone, usually an unknown caller. Why?"

Shit. He was really hoping for more information. "I'd like to know what father is up to and he keeps calling and blustering, but I don't know where he is."

"As long as it's just his nonsense yelling, then it's not too bad. At least he hasn't shown up here again in a while," Catherine offered.

"I'm worried he will. I have nothing to back that up, but I'd like to know where he is. It would tell me if I need to be on guard or not." All of that was true, even if he left some of his concerns out.

"I'll press mother the next time she calls and I answer. You can always use Ryker's hacker guy," she said.

Cade laughed. He already had. "You know he has a name, right?"

"Yep. Hacker guy."

He rolled his eyes at his sister. "That's not it, and you know better."

"He said I can call him that so there."

"You're just doing that to try to get to Ryker." His sister had been interested in Ryker since the first time she met him. Hell, it had been obvious to anyone and still was, for that matter. Ryker didn't give her the time of day, though.

"I'm going to go back to my job now. I'll let you know if I find anything out about where they are."

She let herself out, leaving the door to his office wide open just to piss him off. He got up and closed the door back before returning to his desk and opening the email that 'Hacker Guy' had sent him just this morning.

He had looked into April's past and present, trying to decide what he could offer her to get her to agree to his offer. He hadn't really read it before going to her place, thinking that he would offer his name to get her partnership in her law firm and that would be enough. It clearly wasn't.

Now he needed to read it through and figure out how to use it. He didn't want emotions involved, and if it helped his cause to let her think that any of their past was her fault, he'd let her, even if it killed him a little. None of what happened had been her fault. That's why he had left, to keep it from ruining her.

And yet, here he was, willing to look for blackmail to get her to jump into the fire with him, and she wouldn't even see it coming. With April, he knew he could trust her. Nothing about what he'd told her when they were younger had ever come out in a paper or anything else. She'd told him it was in their bubble forever, and she had kept her word.

He missed her, too. It hurt to admit it, but he did. Most days, he could avoid letting his mind wander down memory lane, but after their date, he couldn't seem to push her back down in that place where he stored his regrets, far from the front of his mind.

Perhaps more accurate was the fact that he missed who he was with her. Back then, being around her had helped wash away all of the drama in his life and he felt cared for. If he could do it all over again, he wouldn't leave her. At the time, his young mind had believed that what he was doing was for the best.

Looking back, he knew that they would have found a way to make everything work. April wouldn't have left him just because of his father's threats, even if they weren't empty ones. He absolutely would have made it impossible for April to get a job and maybe even had her kicked out of school.

Cade had his own money even then and could have supported them until his father came to his sense and even moved them to a new school. He should have at least talked to her, and that was the main reason he didn't explain what happened to her now. She'd be upset with him, and he didn't blame her.

He wanted her to commit to the agreement before explaining so she couldn't back out. She was going to yell at him and he was ready to take all her anger just to have her back for a short while.

Plus the added bonus of making a baby. He wanted her. That much was true. He knew, without a single doubt, that they would be great together if either one of them let it happen. Years ago, he didn't make the move, scared it would ruin what they had. As an adult, he knew better. It would only improve it.

Mind made up, Cade rolled his shoulders and grabbed his phone. One phone call was about to change the trajectory of both of their paths. April was a workaholic and while he could relate, she wasn't yet at the top of her company, but she was well on her way. He could advance that like he told her.

It was time to force her hand.

"Hello, is this Mark?" Cade asked into the phone.

"This is him. How can I help you?"

"I wanted to talk to you about your employee, April."

The man on the other line took a sharp breath.

"It's nothing bad," Cade soothed. "I just wanted to make sure she remembered to put in her time off request."

"Umm, I'm sorry. I can't discuss that with you, sir," Mark said sternly. "That is a private matter and we do respect our employee's privacy."

"I'd imagine that she has more than enough time banked for our honeymoon, but I was worried she'd be too concerned about her career to take the time off, you see? I was hoping that you could help me with making sure she has the dates off?"

There was a pause on the other line. The man knew he was talking to Cade. His secretary would have announced it to him.

"I know she really didn't want our marriage to weigh on her potential move to partner. You know how she is, always wanting to make sure she gets through on her own hard work. Which I'm sure she has, but I really want to make sure we can enjoy our honeymoon."

Cade had him against a wall. They did so much business with the firm that the man wouldn't be able to refuse the request. He chose his words carefully, mentioning the promotion to let the other man know that he knew what influence he had.

"Sorry. I was just surprised. April hasn't told me much about her private life, usually keeping everything separate. I am surprised that you two are engaged. When's the big day?"

"Next week," Cade said, leaving no room for change in his tone.

"I think we can find someone to cover her for two weeks. I'll have to clear this with her, of course."

"Of course. I would expect nothing less. I'm sure she won't be happy that I interfered, but I want to make sure we get a little time to ourselves after the wedding. We are doing a very small ceremony because neither of us wanted it to turn into a spectacle."

"I can only imagine what it would be like," he assured Cade.

"I trust you to keep this between us until April is ready to make her announcement?"

"Of course."

They said their goodbyes and Cade ended the call, leaning back in his chair and waiting for the drama to unfold. April was going to be mad, but hopefully she'd not want to back out. He was manipulating her a bit, but they'd make up eventually and it would all be worth it.

Chapter Eleven
April

Two days later, and April was still fuming about her conversation with Cade and his proposal. She hadn't discussed it with anyone, which was probably why she couldn't move forward, but she wouldn't betray his trust in giving her the reason for his ask. She knew who she was and if she told part of the story, she'd tell it all.

Stewing was an understatement. Her frustration with him and herself was simmering below the surface of everything that she did and it was starting to show. Yesterday she had left work on time, which might as well be early, all because of the fact that one more stupid question was going to send her over the edge.

"What is wrong with me?" she muttered to herself.

"Everything okay?" Mark asked, poking his head into her office.

April nodded. "Just having a moment. I think I might be catching a cold, but I'm trying to keep it at bay," she answered.

Mark took a step back, as though he might get sick from being too close. "Yes, well. I wanted to stop by and say that I think you're making a good move with your engagement, and it will certainly help you grow your clients. If you need to, take the day off but make sure that you still complete your work this weekend, but I know you'll get it done."

April frowned, not liking where this was going. "What are you talking about?" She clenched her fists below her desk as she waited for the answer.

"I spoke with Cade this morning. I must say that I'm a little disappointed that I didn't hear it from you, but I'm happy for you either way. This will be an advantageous marriage for you and the firm." He grinned as though she had done it at his request.

She had done nothing, actually. "I do believe I'll take the day." April made a show of fake coughing and covering her mouth with her open palm.

Mark, as expected, took another step back. "Yes, umm, you do that." He scurried off, likely going to grab his aerosol disinfectant to chase her out of the office with.

Shocked, yet not at the same time, she put her laptop away in her bag and headed out. It was time to confront Cade and have him fix whatever the hell he had done here. She rushed out of the office, ignoring the sound of the disinfectant following behind her.

Safely inside the elevator, she pulled her phone out, dialing Cade. Of course, it went straight to voicemail.

"Cade, you better call me back asap. You cannot force me into what you want. I won't do this." She pressed the end call button with a not so satisfying touch of the screen. She needed the satisfying click of a home phone or a flip phone closing to add emphasis to her emotions right now.

April was fuming when she got into her car to leave. Cade hadn't called her back yet, and she was pretty sure there was steam coming out of her ears at this point.

What right did he have to do this to her when she had no intention of agreeing still? At this point, she was willing to make him look awful to everyone in her office. Maybe she should tell them he had cheated, and that they had to end the engagement? Really, she could say anything she wanted.

Her ride to his office was spent plotting the worst things she could tell her boss about him and why the engagement had to end. She drew the line at saying he'd harmed her. She wasn't about to falsify claims of him hurting her, but cheating was still on the table.

It seemed the entire city was against this rage fueled ride. The normal traffic was only worsened today by her agitated mood and the amount of construction she ran into. She probably should have taken it as a sign that she shouldn't continue this path, but refused to accept it. He had this coming.

Finally pulling up, she allowed another petty thought to creep into reality. She introduced herself to the valet and told them that Cade was paying to park her car. It was less than a drop in the bucket of his money, but it was feeling good until he said he needed to call Cade to confirm.

"No, no. That's okay. I'll just pay. I don't want to disturb his meetings," April backed out of her previous claim of Cade paying.

"Is there a problem?" Catherine jumped into the conversation.

April took her in. She wished she could pull off a white skirt suit. Never would she ever, for fear she'd spill something on it, or worse. Not Catherine. She was the most put-together person April had ever met.

"This woman here claims that she is to put her parking on Mr. Hawkins' bill. I offered to verify that, and she suddenly changed her mind." He looked over at April like he knew she was lying and Catherine was about to tell her off.

Catherine smiled and touched the man on the shoulder. "I can confirm that her parking should go on Cade's bill. Not like it matters anyway, because I'm pretty sure that he gets it free. Please handle her car with the utmost care."

April's jaw dropped as she processed Catherine's words. Catherine reached out and took April's keys from her hand and dropped them in the waiting valet's.

"Come on, April." Catherine turned to walk away before turning back to the stunned and sufficiently shamed valet. "And see that she is added to the list. I would hate to have Cade interrupted for something as simple as a parking issue when you already have the information you need."

April scrambled to catch up with Catherine's long strides and keep her composure. She almost needed to run to keep up, but finally stepped into the elevator with her.

"Come with me to my office," Catherine whispered to her as others joined them on the elevator.

April nodded and swallowed. She knew Catherine was a force to be reckoned with, and it was terrifying to wonder what Catherine wanted with her.

Silently, April stepped out and followed Catherine to her office. While she'd been here before, it was never outside of a conference room and as she followed Catherine, she couldn't help but feel as though she were being walked to the principal's office.

"Have a seat." Catherine gestured to one of the white chairs in her office. "This won't take long."

April cringed inwardly but did take a seat. "Thank you for helping me out there."

Catherine waved her off. "Please, the least he can do is pay for your parking."

Did she know? She knew they were close, but would he have told her about the arrangement he was trying to force on her?

"I know my brother is up to something, and I am not going to ask you what. I also know who you are to him and I find it interesting that my brother is struggling to keep you in his life right now." Catherine took a seat behind her glass desk and rested her elbows on it as she leaned forward. "What I want to know is, what do you want?"

Stunned, April didn't have an answer ready.

"Well, I'll take conflicted over a hard no any day of the week. Next question, are you upset with him right now?" Catherine's smile was growing.

April nodded. "Very." On this, she could undoubtedly answer

any day of the week. She was going to rip him to shreds when she made it up there.

"And he doesn't know you're here?"

"No. But he might have an idea I am coming."

"One second." Catherine pulled up her phone and typed in it. "I'm just checking to see if he's in a meeting or not. I'll restrain myself from following you up and witnessing what I am sure is about to be an amazing show."

"Umm. Thanks?" April said.

"Interesting." Catherine gave her a conspiratorial smile. "He doesn't have any more meetings today. Do you know where you're going?"

April nodded again.

"I will leave you to it, then. Here is my card. My personal cell is on the back. Call me if you need anything, but especially if it's revenge on my hardheaded brother."

She took the card. "I'm not sure what to make of all this," she confessed.

"Me either, but it's intriguing."

April left the woman at her desk and headed back for the elevator. There was something touching about that encounter because she believed that Catherine would have her back if she needed it, and that was weirdly comforting coming from his sister.

Chapter Twelve
Cade

Cade studied the information on his computer screen. There had to be something that he could use to find his parents. He needed to find them and the fact that they could hide this well was blowing his mind.

He needed to know how close his father was to him and what resources he may have access to. It would change everything to locate him.

Catherine had called just a few minutes ago to let him know she wasn't able to get anything from their mother when she called. As a matter of fact, her mother had been offended when Catherine had pressed her about where they were. Thinking it was odd, Catherine had called him right away.

Not wanting to let her in on what was going on yet, Cade just told her he'd keep looking into it. She didn't buy his nonchalance about it, but she let it go. He was trying to protect her from the fallout that was coming once it came out that their father was behind all of this.

Cade's phone vibrated on the desk in front of him. A slow grin spread across his face as April's name flashed across the screen. She knew what he'd done, no doubt.

"Lauren," Cade called from his chair to her. "You can take the rest of the day off after you clear my schedule."

She didn't respond via intercom, instead she walked into his office. "Why?"

"You get a day off, with pay, just take it," he told her.

Lauren put her hands on her hips. "You look like the cat who ate the canary. What did you do?" she asked.

Cade shook his head. "For once since getting with Jake, would you just not question me and carry on with what I asked? You know, that job I pay you to do?"

"You like when I question you. That's why I even have this job, so that I'm not your 'yes man.' You told me that." She rolled her eyes.

"I have other company coming and I would like a bit of privacy, Lauren. Happy?"

"Not even close. Who is coming?"

"You're overstepping, Lauren."

"I'll tell your sister, Cade." She tapped her foot as though she were impatient.

"April," Cade conceded.

"Maybe I should stick around and video her tearing you a new one. I know that the two of you go way back."

"Naturally, the glares and silent treatment gave me some clue that you knew things. Please, cancel my meetings and I'll see you tomorrow." Cade let his eyes go back to his computer screen. He didn't comprehend a single word on the screen, but it told Lauren in no uncertain terms that she was dismissed.

He was rewarded when Lauren walked out of his office, muttering to herself. He didn't catch it, but knew it was something negative about him. It was a good thing they were all friends, and he knew she didn't hate him in the end. She was right that he had hired her because she had challenged him some.

She wasn't defiant, but if he needed an honest opinion, she

always gave it. Since dating Jake, she had grown in her confidence and he no longer had to ask for her opinion. She always gave it.

"That's it." Lauren's voice came through the intercom. "I moved everything. I went ahead and blocked off tomorrow, just in case."

"Thank you. Please take the day with pay."

"Oh, you can bet I am."

Thinking the conversation was over, Cade went back to his computer, looking for any reason to still be here when April showed up. He had no way of knowing that she would show up here, but his gut was rarely wrong and be felt like she was on his way to him.

His patience was rewarded when less than an hour after Lauren left, April showed up. Security questioned if she was allowed up and Cade, of course, told them she was. Apparently, there had been some issues with parking that Catherine had handled, but they wanted to be certain that all was well. Then he went to the elevator to meet her.

As the doors slid open, April stepped out, nearly walking right into him before she looked up. Her eyes were on the ground, paying no attention to where she was going, but still in a hurry.

"Woah," Cade said. He reached out to steady her as they almost collided.

April swayed as she came to an abrupt stop, but recovered. "C-Cade," she said, clearly surprised that he met her at the elevator.

"The one and only," Cade teased with a wink. It was time to turn his charm all the way up and convince this woman to marry him so he could buy some time to find his father and stop this.

April picked at an invisible piece of lint on her skirt, not looking at him, even though she was only an arm's length away. He took a step back and gave her some room. While he was playing a dangerous game with a very thin line of right and wrong by getting her to marry him, he didn't intend into actually force her to anything.

"I need to talk to you, now," April said, her strength growing as she rose her head to lock eyes with him.

This was who he wanted to marry, the woman that would stare

him down. He wanted her to challenge him, he decided. It was why he'd cleared his day, even if he didn't realize the reason then.

"Come into my office," Cade told her.

April nodded and Cade rested one hand on the small of her back to guide her into his office. He heard her sharp intake of breath at the contact and knew he was on the right path with her. She was affected by him as he was by her.

As they entered his office, Cade closed the door behind them and broke the contact between them. He felt the loss much more than he expected, instantly wanting to touch her again.

"What can I help you with?" Cade asked as he clasped his hands behind his back to keep from giving in and touching her again.

April took a moment to gather her words and Cade patiently waited, taking in the petite woman in front of him. She had changed little over the years. She had blossomed from a young adult into a woman, and mostly carried herself as such, but he would know her anywhere.

Her dark hair only accented her big brown eyes. She was shorter than him, but when she spoke, she was unafraid of his much larger self.

"How the hell could you just go ahead and tell my boss that I'm marrying you? You have no right to do such things and now I'm going to look like an idiot when we don't get married. What is wrong with you?" April paced and shouted.

"I told you what I wanted," he said calmly.

"I asked you for one thing, Cade. Your refusal to answer ended the idiotic path I was on by even considering your proposal." She pointed a finger at him. "You think that you can twist me around into a corner and make me do what you want? I asked one thing, just a little bit of honestly." What had started as shouting had slowly dropped to a whisper.

"My father," Cade admitted. "My father was the reason I left, and I thought I was doing the right thing for you."

"That doesn't make sense," April told him.

"Have a seat." Cade gestured to the empty chair as he walked around his desk and took his own seat, needing to put the distance between them if he was going to come clean. "I want to be clear that nothing I say here can leave this room."

"I don't run my mouth," she said, offended.

"My father didn't like that. We were so close. It didn't matter when we were just friends before or dating later on, he didn't like you. You already know the man didn't like me much as it was, so it's not a reflection of you. He thought you were a distraction and looking to get your hands on my money," Cade added an eye roll at that.

April held up her palm for him to stop. "I would never."

"I know. At no point did I ever believe him, but that's not the point. He threatened me, but he also threatened you if I didn't end things." Cade wanted to leave it there, but she shook her head.

"Threatened how?" April asked.

"He was going to stop your financial aid, stop your enrollment, stop you from being able to work. The thing is, he was capable of it." Hopefully, this would be enough because she didn't need to know that he'd also threatened her family and close friends.

"You should have told me," April whispered.

"We weren't the same people then. At least I know I wasn't. I didn't want you to convince me not to make the change. I needed to get away from you and keep all the toxic shit that was my family from touching you. I respected and loved you too damn much to let you get dragged down for me."

"Cade," April sighed. "It truly never occurred to you that I might have been willing to have that fight alongside you instead of you doing it alone?"

"It did, for a moment. Then there were all the thoughts of what if you changed your mind? What if you walked away? What if things got worse than I thought? So I left. I cut you out and kept you safe."

That was more than he ever intended to tell her, even if they got married. The trouble with him was that when it came to April, he didn't know how to shut up. She made him want to keep talking and tell her everything.

April was quiet as he sat there waiting for her to say anything. Just when he thought she was going to say anything, she stood instead.

Cade scrambled up from his own seat. This wasn't going how he expected. April didn't look at him as she went to his office door and opened it. Just before she could cross the threshold and leave him there alone, she turned to face him.

"I'll draw up a contract. Let me know when the wedding will be. After this, you better not ask me for anything else in your whole life. I will have custody of any children from this marriage. To me and see that it is not negotiable." April met his eyes. "Do not call my work again."

Cade hurried a nod. "Deal. We will have the wedding this weekend and then we will take a honeymoon."

"A honeymoon isn't necessary. This is a contract," April reminded him.

"No one else knows that, so it is."

"Fine. I don't know if I can take that long off, but I'll let you know."

"You already have that time," Cade told her. His confidence returning now that she had agreed to help him.

She shook her head. "Of course I do."

April turned to leave and Cade followed her out. "I'll walk you down," he told her.

She opened her mouth to argue, and he watched the emotions that played out on her face. She wanted to rail at him at first, changing to a quiet acceptance. Deciding not to argue, she simply continued to walk to the elevator, leaving Cade to follow behind her.

Chapter Thirteen
April

April sat on her first private jet and couldn't help but look around in wonder. She was hardly raised broke, but she wasn't private jet rich. Her parents had worked hard to give her what they had, and that had left no time for things like vacations.

She wondered if Cade would remember that she had never been on a plane before. Then, he wouldn't know that she still hadn't gotten on a plan in the time between them seeing each other and now, but she hadn't. The entire experience was outside of anything she had ever dreamed of.

Her dreams were ordinary things. Being debt free, marrying someone you get along with, a few kids, a nice house, just the typical thing that most people wanted. Cade made her want other things, passion being the main one.

Without him, her dreams were boring. With him, she questioned her own mind because she wasn't wild and crazy, but that was what she wanted. She wanted to lean over and kiss him. She wanted him to take her to the back of the plane and make her a member of the mile high club.

"I swear on everything I hold dear that I am trying to behave myself around you, but if you look at me like that one more time, then I am not going to be responsible for my own actions." Cade shifted in his seat and adjusted his pants.

April bit her lip as Cade groaned. She turned her head to look out the window instead. This whole trip was an involuntary lust trap. Every time he said something like that, she only got more turned on than she already was.

"Did you ever get a chance to travel?" Cade asked.

She shook her head. "Haven't had the time."

"So, this is your first plane ride?" Cade asked her.

"Yep." April held her breath to see how he reacted to that news.

"Well, you're doing it in style. This is way better than an economy flight to anywhere." He leaned over in his seat so they were both looking out of the window.

Cade sat across from her and they were now almost face to face as they both looked out of the same window.

"Are you nervous?" Cade asked.

"About you or the plane?" she squeaked.

He arched one eyebrow at her. "Both?"

April quickly nodded her head and resisted the urge to push harder against the back of her seat and hide. It wasn't fear. No, it was excitement, but uncertainty.

"You let me know when you're not," Cade said simply and backed away from her.

April sat, stunned, waiting for the man to come back, but he didn't. She wanted him to kiss her, to touch her, to anything. She was screwed, and they weren't even married yet.

They were on their way to Vegas to make that happen quickly.

Confused and not the smallest bit overwhelmed, she looked out the window and watched as Vegas came into view. It was beautiful from up here, watching the town magically appear in what had been nothing but desert.

"Buckle up, babe," Cade told her.

April ignored the endearment, not quite sure it was actually that or more of a joke. Her heart lept at the word, but she pushed that thought aside as she buckled herself in.

Joking and teasing wasn't the side of Cade she expected to see at any point, much less on their way to do this sham of a marriage. She wasn't prepared to handle it, hadn't even considered that Cade might not be cranky about this situation. He was always short with everyone according to anyone she talked to, even his sister, but not right now.

Rather than comment on it, April took it as a win and just let whatever was going to happen, happen. This chipper mood wouldn't last, she knew, so what was the harm in enjoying it?

"Did you need to change or anything?" Cade asked as the plan landed.

April looked down at her current outfit. Probably not something she wanted to get married in, as there would no doubt be some pictures of today. Jeans and a baggy shirt weren't wedding wear.

She nodded. "If you don't mind? I can change in the bathroom."

Cade laughed. "If you manage that in this small bathroom, I'll be impressed. You can take that door all the way to the back. It's a bedroom you can use."

April took her one suitcase and made her way to the door. She made quick work of changing into a white summer dress she'd packed. It was the most wedding-like dress she owned while also keeping things casual, which was what Cade wanted.

"All ready?" Cade knocked on the door.

"Coming," April called back.

A small mirror was just enough to fix her hair and put on some simple eye makeup. Not one to wear a lot, anyway. She didn't see the need to do a ton today, just a simple bit on her eyes, and she was ready.

Cade was on the other side of the door still when she pulled it open. He grabbed her hand, not commenting on the dress, and practically dragged her from the plane.

"My bag," April said.

"It will be in the room later," he assured her.

With no choice but to follow, April let it go. He opened the door to a car for her, waving off the driver who was there to do just that. She slid in and they were off without another word.

They hadn't discussed where the wedding would happen and she regretted that, as she didn't know what to expect.

"Where are we going?" April asked.

"To the chapel," Cade answered.

She rolled her eyes. "What kind of chapel?"

"A wedding one."

"Fine." April folded her arms and sat back in the seat. If he didn't want to talk, then she wouldn't make him.

Ten awkwardly silent minutes later, the car came to a stop. "We're here," Cade said before opening the door and getting out of the car.

April slid across the seat, taking a deep breath to calm the nerves that were rising up before she put her hand in Cade's and stood.

She was really doing this, her brain repeated. She was going to marry Cade, and why? That was the million-dollar question, wasn't it? Was she marrying him because she was an idiot who still wasn't over young love? Probably. Was she just someone who was too nice and willing to do whatever he wanted to help? Also likely.

The only question that mattered was if she was going to regret this. She looked down at their connected hands and knew there was little chance that she would not regret this.

April stood quietly by while Cade spoke and filled out paper-work, only stepping forward to sign her name when she was called. As a contract lawyer, she should know enough to read anything she was being asked to sign, but here she was, writing her signature on everything with no one clue as to what it was.

"You good?" Cade asked.

She pasted on her best fake smile and nodded.

Cade gave her a look that said he didn't believe her, but didn't press. As they finished, a woman came and led April to another area.

"You'll wait here until your future husband is in place and then you can walk down the aisle," she explained.

Her big hair, which shook as she talked animatedly about the different veils that were available for her to choose from, fascinated April.

"Did you hear me, hun?" she asked.

"I'm sorry, what?" April asked, pulling herself out of the 6-inch tall hair and back to Earth. "I was lost in my thoughts."

"No worries. Getting married is a big deal, and it can make some people a little nervous." She proceeded to hand her a veil.

"Thank you, but I think I'm good."

"You have to pick one. Your man paid for the big package. He said you needed to have a real wedding," she explained.

She wanted to melt, but the reality was that it was just him trying to make sure there were good photos that came from this sham of a marriage. Taking the veil the woman held out, April set it on her head, letting the floral halo rest in her own hair.

"Perfect," the woman gushed. "It matches your dress! Now, you'll walk down the aisle slowly, and we will have a photographer out there taking your pictures. Then you'll say your vows, exchange your rings, and that will be that."

The lump in her throat made it hard to swallow. This was really real and now things were different. SHe also hadn't thought about a ring for either of them.

"I don't have a ring," April whispered.

"Don't worry about it. Your man already handed them over, so it's already out there for the ceremony." If the woman thought any of this was weird, she didn't let on. "Now, it's your time to shine."

She threw back heavy black curtains and April was suddenly in a chapel setting, looking down the aisle at Cade. Her feet froze and she couldn't move forward, no matter how hard she tried.

Trembling, she watched as Cade's face went from smiling to

confusion before she stepped away from the arch and walked towards her. She expected frustration from him, or maybe even anger, but what she didn't see coming was the tenderness in his gaze as it met hers.

"You don't have to do this," Cade told her. A completely different tune from the man that had pulled out all the stops to get her here.

"I can't," April started.

"Can't do this?" Cade asked.

She shook her head again. "I can't move." It was like the nerves had paralysed her and there was no way she could go forward or backwards, stuck in limbo at the entrance.

"I can carry you?" he offered.

It was that, or they didn't get married today. She nodded and wrapped her arms around his neck as he lifted her bridal style and carried her down the aisle.

"Everything okay?" the officiant asked.

"All good. Just a bit of cold feet," Cade assured him.

"I'm sorry. I don't know what came over me." She made an attempt at a laugh but it came out as awkward as she felt.

"Let's begin, then."

She listened as he spoke and repeated the words when she was told Cade did the same. It was going well until he slid a ring on her finger and the weight of the decisions she'd made hit her in full. The ring was gaudy, heavy, showy, everything she wasn't and wouldn't want. It only served to remind her how fake this all was.

"You may kiss the bride," she heard as Cade leaned forward.

She didn't need to be nervous. She was doing him a favor. All the reassuring thoughts went through her mind as Cade's lips met hers.

Chaste, this kiss was not. As his tongue slipped past her lips, April let him. Just this once, she was going to let herself enjoy it just this once and pretend that Cade wanted her. She felt herself leaning into him as Cade pulled her closer.

Cheering came from the back of the room and Cade broke the

kiss, tucking her against him. "What the hell?" His gruff voice was strained.

April twisted in his grasp and turned away from his shirt to see what was going on. There, at the other end of the aisle, was Cade's entire friend group cheering and celebrating.

"I didn't know they would come. I don't know how they knew," Cade whispered into her hair.

"Friends of the happy couple?" the officiant asked.

"They were," Cade grunted.

Chapter Fourteen
Cade

Cade buttoned his shirt and cursed his friends. How they found out what he was up to, he didn't know, but he wanted a little bit of time with April before they needed to pretend to be a happy couple. She was nervous as it was, and this wasn't helping things.

Granted, she knew most of his friends and was close with Evan's girlfriend, but this hadn't been planned, and he hated when shit went sideways.

April showered as he got ready in their room. They had been roped into going out to celebrate with everyone this evening, and he hated it. He hated that they'd interrupted and that while he wanted to take this time to break down some of April's shield. He was going to be forced to pretend there were none.

"Cade?" April's quiet voice came through the crack in the bathroom door. "I... umm..."

"What is it?" Cade bit out, a lot more angry than he meant to be with her ever. He cleared his throat and tried again. "Sorry. I'm just frustrated. What's wrong?"

"I just forgot something in my bag. If you let me know when you're ready to leave the room, I'll get it when you're done."

"What is it? I'll get it for you." Cade moved to her suitcase, sitting on the bed.

"I'll get it," April assured him. "I'm just not dressed yet."

Already annoyed at everything, Cade turned to the door. "What is it, April? We don't have long until we are meeting everyone, so just tell me what you need."

"Umm, my panties. They're on the top. Any pair will do," she rushed out.

Cade groaned. This was what he got for pressing. He should have walked away like she wanted and he wouldn't be pulling out a pair of black thongs to hand to April. To be fair, that was the first pair he grabbed.

He pictured her on the other side of the door, likely beet red with embarrassment, as Cade pressed the garment into her waiting hand that was sticking through the cracked door.

"Thanks," she muttered as the door clicked closed behind her.

Cade dropped onto the bed and sighed. Today wasn't going as he needed it to. She hadn't told him if she was willing to create a baby the natural way and he wanted to seduce her, now he'd embarrassed her and he wasn't going to get to recover from that today.

He'd booked one room for the two of them and made sure to get a king bed so they'd have to share. If she stuck to herself, he wouldn't push her. He needed her to want to come to him, but he'd make sure she knew what she was missing out on.

"I'm ready," April said as she opened the door.

Cade stood and walked to the bedroom door, slipping into his shoes. "Let's go."

April walked past him, a dress that hugged her curves melded to her body. His punishment for not just leaving the room earlier would be that he knew why he couldn't see her panty lines and exactly what was on under that dress.

As though feeling his gaze, she turned to look at him. "Are you coming?"

"Just enjoying the view," he teased.

April's face turned red this time, and he caught a whiff of her perfume as she whipped her head around to walk away from him. The suite was large enough, more like a small apartment, and he caught up to her before she reached the door.

"We were worried you weren't going to come see us!" Lauren jumped up when they made it to the lobby and hugged April.

"Just trying to get ready," April answered.

"Didn't see this coming," Jake slapped Cade on his back as he spoke. "Anything you want to tell me?"

Cade shook his head. "We knew each other before. I just realized I didn't want to go too long without knowing her again," he tried.

Jake rolled his eyes. "You're full of shit."

Cade was saved from replying to that accurate statement by Evan and Ryker approaching. "Congrats, man." Evan slapped his back harder than Jake.

Ryker eyed him but didn't say anything.

"Where's Luke?" Cade asked. He couldn't imagine Luke passing up a chance to be in Vegas.

Ryker grunted and raised his arm, pointing off by the front desk where Luke was flirting with a blond woman in a tight red dress.

"Figures," Cade said with a shrug.

"Everyone ready?" Kayla asked the group before her gaze landed on Luke. "Ugh. Someone get him."

Cade bit back a laugh. He wasn't sure how else she expected Luke to act. This was him ten times out of ten.

"I'll do it." Ryler walked over, squeezed his hand on the back of Luke's neck and dragged him back to the group. "Got him."

"Okay. So first we want to have dinner, obviously," Kayla started.

"I want to ride the Ferris wheel," Lauren added.

"Let's get started then." Jake led the group out of the hotel and onto the brightly lit Vegas strip.

Cade

The group made their way to a restaurant. Cade didn't notice the walk or much of the scenery. What he did notice was April. Her eyes were wide as she took in the sights, pointing at things and talking to Kayla and Lauren.

Her eyes were lit up and she looked very much like she did before he left her. Wide-eyed and ready to take on the world while taking it all in. He hadn't realized how much that brightness was gone until now, when he could see it returned.

He couldn't help but wonder if the lack of light in her had been his fault. It seemed selfish that he might have been the cause of her disillusionment while also heartbreaking. He genuinely hoped that none of this was simply because he was an idiot in his youth.

"What?" April looked up at him as they walked.

"Just looking at you," he said.

She blushed and ducked her head. "Stop. It's weird."

"It's not weird. You're my wife." Using the tip of his index finger, he pressed lightly below her chin, urging her to look up. "Maybe I want to look at my wife," he told her.

April held his gaze until Lauren interrupted them. "You have a lifetime with her. We are here to have fun this weekend," she sang out and pulled April away from him.

It didn't escape his notice that everyone seemed to be pulling them apart. Well, not everyone, but the women at least were keeping April from being glued to his side, where he wanted her.

They all sat around a large table, the women together and Cade opposite April, who was definitely avoiding his gaze.

"Come clean," Ryker said. "Why did you do it?"

"I don't know what you mean," Cade said.

"I know that you've been using my employee to look for people, Cade. I know that you and April may have been a thing before, but you haven't spent any time together of significance until tonight. I know a lot more than you think I do." Ryker's eyes never left the other side of the room as he spoke to Cade right next to him.

Cade sat silently. He didn't know what to say to his friend, but he knew he was getting close to being directly called out. "There's a lot here that you don't know," Cade admitted.

Ryker let out a harsh laugh. "Isn't that what I just said?"

"Maybe."

"When you get back, I expect answers and to know how we can help. You know whatever it is, we will help you." Ryker turned and held Cade's gaze for a beat before letting it go.

Cade blew out a breath. Was it too much to just ask one thing in his life to go right? He mused.

"Are you explaining to him how a wedding night works?" Luke leaned over between Cade and Ryker.

"Man, don't start your shit. She's right there and doesn't need to be embarrassed by you," Cade snapped at his friend.

Luke grunted and stood up. "You really did it, didn't you?" he asked.

"Did what?" Cade took a sip of the water in front of him.

"You actually got married. Never thought I'd see you cave."

As Luke returned to his own seat, Cade wondered if Luke knew more than what he let on. Brushing off the thought, he laughed to himself. Luke wasn't in on this. It was just his nonsense about not wanting a relationship with anyone.

Luke was like that, always giving them a hard time about not wanting his lifestyle of chaotic one-night stands. They'd all been through that phase in one way or another, and everyone except Luke had outgrown that time in their lives.

Dinner was a loud affair. Everyone laughed and joked, clearly having a good time. No one brought up their suspicions of Cade's motive for the wedding and in the end, he finally relaxed.

"We have something for you," Jake stood, getting everyone's attention. "not that you can't afford it or anything." He rolled his eyes and everyone laughed. "But we thought that the two of you might want to get away for a little while."

Jake held up an envelope and handed it to April. Cade got up and walked behind her, curious as to what was in it.

April gasped as she pulled out an itinerary. It seemed that everyone had gotten together and planned a honeymoon for them to the south of France. He enjoyed it there and while he had something else in mind, April seemed happy with this trip.

"Thank you," Cade said to Jake.

"It was all of us, but you're welcome," Jake laughed. "We wanted to make sure that you both got to spend some time together before returning to work. Knowing you, the plan was probably to be back to work on Monday."

"Actually," Cade cleared his throat. "She was the one that I had to convince to take the time off. I was more than ready to take a honeymoon."

"Well, you two are a matching pair," Evan moaned.

They paid and left, heading for the Ferris wheel. April was oddly quiet now that she was walking alongside him and not with her friends. She had let him take her hand though and to anyone looking at them, they would appear as a happy couple who were just taking in the night.

Cade knew her mind was racing. It was all over her face as different thoughts ran through it. She was never good at hiding what she was thinking. He'd often teased her she needed to fix that before she finished her degree and became a lawyer.

It was the one place she did hide it. Or time, rather. When she was working, and he'd seen it a few times, she was able to keep a mask in place. Even seeing her for the first time when the restaurant was in trouble, he'd had a hard time hiding his surprise. April though, her eyes had widened a fraction and then she'd got herself under control again. If he hadn't been watching so hard, he probably wouldn't have noticed her slight surprise.

"Well, some of us have to work tomorrow," Jake laughed.

"Since when do you work?" Cade joked back.

"Well, I was talking about Evan," he shrugged.

The whole group laughed.

They made it back to the hotel and said they're good nights to each other and headed to their own rooms. April was quiet as they made it to their room and mumbled something before quietly slipping into the bathroom.

82

Chapter Fifteen
April

April locked herself in the bathroom, leaning against the security of the door behind her as she took several deep breaths. She was alone with Cade now, as husband and wife, with one bed.

He surely would not do the gentlemanly thing and offer to sleep elsewhere, and she could hardly rent another room. She also wasn't about to sleep on the hotel floor. Didn't matter how nice and clean this one looked. It was a public-ish floor, and she wasn't sleeping on it.

There was the sofa in the sitting area, though. Smiling to herself, April stood. It was a solid, good plan. In the meantime, she was going to avail herself of this amazing shower and enjoy it, knowing the hot water would not run out.

Her apartment was far from a disaster, but her hot water was glitchy. Sometimes she got five minutes, others she got thirty. Tonight it was forever.

Trying to shake that thought from her head since it related to more than hot water in her life right now, she undressed and stepped in, letting the near scalding water cascade over her skin. She would absolutely be red when she stepped out, but it was going to be worth it.

In the end, she didn't know how long she enjoyed the shower, but only after she wrapped herself in her towel did she remember her bag was in the room where Cade was likely waiting for her. She tucked the towel closed and padded to the door, hoping he was in the other room.

Peeking out the door was greeted by emptiness. Not quite relaxed but feeling better, she reached into her suitcase, grabbing a few things and dashing back to the bathroom before he came in.

It didn't take long to get dressed, and she wrapped her hair in a towel before opening the bathroom door fully and stepping out, more confident now. Cade was still not in the room and she wondered how long she had actually been in there.

"Might as well find him," she muttered to herself.

Find him, she did. Cade was fast asleep on the small sofa with his feet over one side. His neck resting on the other. She almost felt bad and woke him up. Almost. Instead, she grabbed a blanket from the closet and covered him up before going to bed herself, noting the open bottle of liquor next to him.

Disappointedly, she climbed into the massive bed and stared at the ceiling in the darkness, attempting to sort through her feelings. She didn't know how she felt, but now that nothing was going to happen, she couldn't deny the disappointment that her wedding night was going to be spent alone with her new husband passed out, likely drunk, in the other room.

She was a mess. Her nerves rattled and feelings for Cade that she'd buried long ago were bubbling to the surface. This was just an arrangement, and she needed to remember that as things progressed and time moved on. Maybe it was better if they went the other route of conception, because the odds of her remembering this weren't real if they slept together were slim.

With a huff, she yanked the covers up to her chin and rolled to her side, away from the door and away from Cade. She wasn't going to lie here and think about how much Cade had acted like his younger self today. It was too hard for her brain to separate fact from fiction.

Briefly, she considered going back out there and stealing the open bottle. A nightcap would likely help settle her wandering thoughts. She didn't want to see Cade again, though, so she remained in the bed.

It wasn't long before she heard Cade moving in the other room. She laid very still and listened as he groaned and approached the room. He wasn't quiet, clearly the alcohol affecting his normal quiet but powerful demeanor.

He opened the door and went to the bathroom, flipping the light on before closing the door. April waited to see if he'd join her or go back to the other room. It felt like forever, but couldn't have been that long before he emerged again. Bright light filling the dark bedroom before flicking back off once more.

She felt the covers pull back and the mattress dip as Cade slid in beside her. April's eyes were open as she faced away from him, unmoving, waiting, anticipating what would happen next. She felt like a damn virgin the way she was worrying about it. She wasn't, of course, but it had been a long time, and never had it been with Cade.

His arm touched her back, and then he pulled away quickly. Had he forgotten she was in here? It quickly returned, hooking around her middle and pulling her against him.

Her back was now flush with his front as he held her. April didn't react until he moaned her name, and she felt his cock stiffen against her. In that instant, she knew there was no resisting him for her. If Cade made a move, she would be putty in his hands.

As though he heard her thoughts and took them as encouragement, Cade's hand slid up and under her shirt, palming her breast. Her sharp intake of breath was stolen again when he began to press kisses to her neck.

Giving up all pretense of being asleep, April rolled over onto her back, giving him better access to all of her. Cade released her then, and she worried that she'd screwed up completely by moving, but he only turned on the small bedside lamp.

"I need to see you," his gravely voice interrupted the silence.

Joining her once more in the bed, his hand returned to her breast and quickly reassured her he wasn't leaving. Insecurities melted away as he lifted her sleep shirt and took one pebbled nipple in his mouth. Thought left entirely as she arched her back, her body begging for more.

"I always knew you'd be responsive." Cade's hands replaced his mouth, both breasts receiving attention.

She marveled at the feel, Cade's rough hands against her soft, sensitive skin. Never had she nearly come from breast play alone, but she felt the pressure building as she grew wetter and ready for him.

He kissed her then, as his hands left her breasts. She let out a whine of protest against his mouth and felt him chuckle in return. Cade's left hand traveled down her body, leaving goosebumps in its wake as anticipation built for what would happen next.

Her sleep shorts were in the way, but he slid under them as though they weren't there. His hand found her soaking wet core and, without preamble, slipped one finger inside.

April cried out, lifting off the bed as she did. Cade kissed her back down on the mattress as his hand explored and teased her. His palm ground against her clit, setting a steady rhythm that was driving her wild.

In minutes, she felt the pressure building until she couldn't take it any longer. Uninhibited, she cried out for him, her arms coming around his back, clinging to him as she soared over the cliff.

Her body shook. Cade didn't pull away from her as she clung to him. Instead, he pressed gentle kisses to her neck as she rode her wave of pleasure back down to Earth. Slowly, she released him as her languid body relaxed against the mattress.

"Are you ready to do that again?" his deep voice sent new tremors through her body with the promise it offered.

"I don't think I can move," April answered him honestly.

"You won't need to much," Cade spoke as he pulled back.

This wasn't the night she had imagined it as something more. Hurried, but not at the same time. April lifted her hips and pulled her clothes off, watching as Cade stood to do the same.

The man was unreal. Every muscle was toned, and she appreciated the movement of each one as he removed his clothes. Freeing his cock from his boxers, it jutted forward.

April gasped as she took him in, completely naked. He wasn't hers, but she couldn't convince her heart to listen to her brain when Cade looked at her, his tongue slipping out and licking his lips like she was a feast and he was a man starved.

Cade reached for his clothes, likely looking for a condom, before turning and grinning at her. Since they were trying to make a baby, there was no need for protection. This would be a first for her, never having had unprotected sex, the thought making her excited all over again.

From the end of the bed, Cade rested both knees on the edge before pushing her legs open and settling above her.

"Are you sure?" he whispered.

It took her a moment to register that he had spoken. She felt his restraint in the slight shake of his arms that were resting next to her head. He was giving her a chance to say no, which was sweeter than she expected, but wholly unnecessary.

"I'm sure," she managed.

"Thank God," Cade answered.

In one swift movement, he positioned himself at her entrance. In the next, he filled her completely.

April yelled his name as she felt him. Unlike anything she'd ever known, she felt full, impossibly so, but unbelievably ready for me. He didn't give her long to adjust to him, but she didn't need it, anyway.

One thing that April had never done before was orgasm from sex alone. As Cade drove into her, she felt her climax rising again. She had no control as Cade set the pace and she was happy to give him complete control.

Quicker than she would have imagined ever possible, April felt her peak nearing. Her feet wrapped around Cade's waist of their own accord, pulling him deeper and deeper still before, finally and still too quickly, she gave over to the pleasure.

Cade followed, roaring out his own climax before dropping back down to his elbows, holding his weight off of her. They were both breathing hard and heavy, a slick layer of sweat covering them both.

She thought he would roll away from her now, sated and sleepy, but in yet another unexpected moment from this man, he only lowered himself beside her. With one arm, he pulled her back up against him, tucking her next to him and pulling the covers over them.

April drifted off to sleep without reminding herself this wasn't real. She didn't think about the fact that she should shower or pull away from this fantasy. Instead, she slept on, feeling safe and protected in his arms.

Chapter Sixteen
Cade

Cade stood in his boxers, drinking coffee in their small kitchen of the hotel room, trying to figure out what happened. All he knew was he woke up naked next to April and scrambled from the bed. They'd had sex. He knew it to his core, but he couldn't remember shit.

Figured that the first time they slept together, he wouldn't even know if either one of them enjoyed it. Did she hate him? She was still in bed, so maybe it wasn't too bad. He just hoped that he had taken care of her before himself in his drunken state.

She'd locked herself in the bathroom for so long last night that he'd opened the bottle of bourbon that Ryker had given him as a wedding present and proceeded to get drunk. Only he wasn't that drunk at first. Then he'd passed out. His last memory was him fighting to keep his eyes open and slowly losing the battle.

He didn't want to wake her, so he'd partially closed the door when he left the room, leaving it open enough to look in and see she was still in bed. She could sleep all day if she wanted. They were on no timeframe right now.

There was the matter of the generous gift of a honeymoon from his friends to settle, though. They probably would not go. First, he didn't know if she even had a passport, and second, he had something planned already.

His phone rang loudly, and he dropped it in his haste to answer. Snatching it off the floor, he pressed answer without noting who the caller was, only seeking to stop the ringing before it work April.

"This is Cade," he said into the phone.

"How many times must I tell you to stop answering the phone like that?" his father's voice came through.

"Shit," Cade didn't even bother to whisper it. This was a call he hadn't wanted to take today.

"I heard that you have been up to something. I was clear about what needed to happen, Cade." The menace is his tone was almost palpable.

"I did what you asked. I got married and am working on the baby part," Cade tried to sound flippant.

"That was not who you were supposed to marry. There is no advantage to that match and you damn well know it," he raged.

"You never said there had to be. You told me to get married and have an heir," Cade reminded him.

"It was implied. You're playing games, son, and I am not to be played with."

"Don't call me son. I stopped being a son to you a long time ago. I did what you asked. Now, slink off into oblivion and leave us all alone."

"Get your ass down to the courthouse and annul that marriage right now, before anyone finds out."

Cade smiled to himself. "Can't. Plus, I had photos sent to the paper to make sure everyone knew this morning."

"No one cares if you fucked her. Just say you didn't. It's Vegas, no one cares. Get this fixed now." He skipped the announcement a bit, clearly choosing not to hear it.

"Why don't you tell me where you are and we can talk man to

man? Frankly, at this point I am sick of being threatened by a voice with no body to it. Until then, you can kiss my ass."

Cade ended the call and dropped his phone on the counter. He needed to do that a long time ago instead of putting up with this shit for this long. He felt like he could finally breathe again and knew part of it was the woman in the other room.

Glancing over, he didn't see her anymore. She'd gotten up and some point during the call, hopefully before she listened to too much of it.

"April?" Cade asked, going in search of the room for her.

"Just a minute," she called from the bathroom.

He was damn tired of her hiding in that bathroom from him. Half the time they'd spent in this room, she'd hidden in there.

"Sorry," she stepped out, a little breathless, but dressed with her face washed and teeth brushed.

Cade smiled at her. He might not remember shit from last night, but she wasn't acting like a woman whose man put his needs before her own. Pushing his luck, he took a step forward and pressed a kiss to her forehead.

"Did you sleep okay?" He asked, pulling her in against his bare chest.

She nodded against him. "I think so."

"We aren't in a rush. Do you want to hang out here today?" Cade offered. It was what he wanted. No need to interrupt what was going so well.

Before she could answer, his phone rang again. He stepped away from April and stormed into the other room, grabbing it off the counter. To his surprise, it wasn't his father again. This time, it was Evan.

He answered with a smile. "Anyone ever tell you not to bother people on their honeymoon?"

"I wish I was just bothering you," Evan sounded serious.

Cade walked back into the room, sitting on the edge of the bed and patting the space next to him, hoping April would join him. "What's wrong?"

"Someone started a fire in the alley last night next to the restaurant. Nothing is damaged, but it definitely was a threat that they could do more if they wanted. It was deliberate, the police said."

"What the fuck?" Cade demanded. "Let me call you back." He hung up on his friend and turned to April.

"What's wrong?" Her eyes were wide as her hand came up to rest on his arm.

"Unfortunately, we need to go. Seems people are up to their old tricks again. I'm going to have to cut the whole trip short. Sorry."

He left her sitting there and went to his suitcase, tossing it on the bed. April moved around the room, getting her things together. In less than half an hour, the plane was ready, and they were closing their bags.

April hadn't said a word as he fumed. He couldn't even find the words to try to fix things with her. He had tried to call his father's bluff and that his father had proven he wasn't bluffing. It was a dangerous game, one Cade was currently losing at.

He was working on his phone in the car on the way to the airport. Despite knowing that he needed to acknowledge April, he couldn't bring himself out of this situation and talk to her. Working quickly was important here, as he had Ryker's man looking for his father.

Cade didn't care where his mother was. If she was involved in this, then it was at his father's insistence. He just needed to find his father and put an end to all this once and for all. The man had money in so many places, probably under aliases, and it was making things hard.

Not once had they caught up to them. They could have been in the same place for the last six months and Cade wouldn't know it. Shit, they could be down the street. Which begs the question of who he had reporting back to him what was going on.

His marriage wasn't a secret, people knew, but it hadn't gone public yet. Something that his father would be pissed about when it did. Cade wasn't taking it back, though. He'd done as he'd been told. His father was just pissed that he'd been outsmarted. The man would just have to get over it.

Cade helped April onto the plane, but outside of a few words here and there, they hadn't spoken still. As they buckled in, Cade leaned forward and rested one hand on her knee.

"We will be home shortly," he told her.

April just nodded and turned her head to look out the window. He let her be and went back to his phone, working just as diligently to find his father as he could. She didn't realize it, but by marrying him she was at more risk that all of his friends, which meant he'd really fucked up.

Now his only goal was to find a way not to need to admit that to her and solve this situation before it blew up on him. April hadn't asked him what was going on, probably knowing he wouldn't answer, so for now, it was on only him to solve it.

She sniffed a few times, and Cade wondered if she was crying. He shrugged it off. Surely there was no way that she was in tears right there beside him. It wasn't until they landed and he went to help her stand that he realized she had been in tears.

"April," he started. He didn't get any further before his phone rang again. "Shit. One second."

Stepping away from her, he put the phone to his ear.

"Fix it," his father demanded. "I know you're looking for me and it won't change a damn thing. Fix this mess you made now and marry the right woman."

"I did exactly what you asked, and that's just going to have to be enough. I will figure out where you are, I guarantee it."

His father's dark laugh came through the phone. "No. You won't. Not until I want you to know where I am."

The call ended and Cade punched at the air, pissed. "Let's go," he said to April, way more harshly than he needed to. She flinched at his tone, and Cade cursed again. When would anything go right in his life again?

Chapter Seventeen
April

No honeymoon was in their future, with no explanation forthcoming. She had spent the rest of the weekend directing people where to put her things as she settled into Cade's home.

What had started out as a great wedding day had dissolved into the coldness she had expected in less than 24 hours. Cade was distant, engrossed in his phone, and hadn't spoken much.

She had also been moved into a spare room next to his. They were not going to live as man and wife behind closed doors, and April had to shove the disappointment down as far as she could.

Nothing had changed about their arrangement because they'd had sex. Even if it was the best sex of her life. The only person to blame for the feelings she'd let back out after so long dormant was herself. She knew what she was signing up for and despite her better judgement, she'd agreed to it.

This morning, she had decided to go back to work. Sitting around idle wasn't in her nature, and she really wasn't going to do it in Cade's house. She hadn't seen him before she left, so she'd sent a text letting him know where she'd be.

Settling back into the monotony of her job after a few days away was just a reminder that she needed to find something else to do. Maybe after this contract marriage was over, she could job hunt more seriously, especially with a child.

Her mind wandered to what that child would look like and how much her life would change when she had a baby. Working at this pace was definitely not doable and she wouldn't want someone else to raise her child for her like so many people in her office did.

"I'm surprised to see you back so soon," Mark appeared at her desk.

April pasted on her best work smile and looked away from the contract she'd been typing. "You know how it is. Work wasn't going to wait, so we will have to honeymoon another time."

"Yes. It's important that you both understand that. It will help you go far. I did hear that your husband is in the building, though. I suppose non-working lunches and early days will be a new thing to expect from you..." he trailed off.

Cade was here? That was news to her. "Unlikely to be a regular thing, I assure you. It's just all so new right now," she told him.

"Yes, well. I did plan on not having you here, so I suppose shorter days for the next week will make sense." He practically choked on his own words.

"April?" Cade's voice interrupted anything she was going to say.

"It's nice to meet you, Mr. Hawkins," Mark stuck out his hand for Cade to shake.

She watched him closely to see if he would let on any sense of disapproval of the man. For some stupid reason, she wanted him not to like Mark either. Cade didn't flinch, unfortunately, as he greeted him and took his hand. She was rewarded slightly when he discreetly wiped his hands on his pants after letting go.

"April, I know we didn't discuss it, but I was hoping we could cut out early today for dinner since our honeymoon was cut short?" he asked, but she knew it wasn't really a question, if Cade was here he wanted something.

Dinner? What time was it? She looked over at the clock and noticed it was already past five. "I think that's a wonderful idea."

She placed her computer in her bag and grabbed the few things she had as Mark and Cade chatted, completely ignoring her.

"Ready?" Cade asked, taking her laptop bag from her.

He must have been paying some attention to her because she'd only just turned around with it and began to stand. "Yep," she said with a forced happiness.

"I will see you tomorrow?" Mark asked.

"That's the plan," she answered.

Cade was by her side the moment she'd stepped from behind her desk. His hand was on the small of her back as he led her out of the office and to the elevator.

"I don't like him much," Cade mumbled. "I didn't care for him on the phone, but in person, even less."

"You hid it well," she told him.

"Yes, I'm good at that."

When he said nothing else, she let the conversation drop. The ride to the ground floor was silent. No one joined them and she wondered if they somehow knew who was on the elevator and gave him special treatment. Not that it was possible, but it still felt like it.

"We can take my car. Cade led her out the front door of the building. We will have someone else come back for yours later."

April didn't reply. What was there to say that would matter? She didn't care about the car, so she slid into the backseat of the waiting car that Cade had led her to. He took the seat next to her and closed the door. In less than a minute, the car was moving.

"While it's just us, I wanted to bring you this to review." He handed her a folder.

April opened it and skimmed the contents. It was the contract for their marriage with more lucrative terms than they'd discussed.

"Cade, this is too much," she started to hand it back.

He held up a hand, stopping her. "Put it in your bag and read through it later. As long as nothing is less than we agreed to, just sign it and I'll have copies made for you."

She nodded and did as he asked. She'd tried to tell him it was too much, but if he didn't care, then maybe she shouldn't argue. Money wasn't going to heal her broken heart at the end of all this, but it would help her and the baby while she looked for a new job.

"What's for dinner?" April asked, changing the subject.

Cade explained about a restaurant that she'd never been to. When he realized that, she got a long spiel on the menu and what was good to eat there. She had no real preferences, so told him to order for her.

It was easier to defer to him, but she also had a feeling she didn't want to look at the menu. While she'd never been there, she knew what it was, and she didn't want to see the prices. It was crazy expensive, and she didn't want to know how much the meal cost that she was about to eat. It went against everything in her to spend a few hundred dollars on one meal.

They had greeted several people on the way to their table that Cade knew. A few she recognized from the news or magazine covers, but no one she personally would have spoken to if it weren't for Cade.

Dinner itself was very good. They made small talk over the meal and the food was delicious. They had a few people stop at their table to meet Cade's new wife, but overall, an easy affair. The walk out was similar to the one end, meeting new people until they made it back to the car.

"I thought it would be good to get out and announce our marriage in person," Cade explained in the car.

"I hope I did okay, then," she told him.

"Of course you did." Cade looked at her like she'd lost her mind. "It was a test, April. It was just letting people know that we are married and we needed to eat, too. I'm sorry that we didn't get to honeymoon, but you didn't have to go back to work."

He changed subjects so quickly. "I don't want to sit around and do nothing."

"Fair enough. Tomorrow, take the car service. I know it may not be what you're used to, but it is safer and if anything ever changes in your day, you can call them at any moment." Cade looked out the window instead of at her when he spoke.

"Okay." This wasn't a hill she was going to die on. Not driving around the city made her life easier, no arguments from her.

They pulled up in front of Cade's house and he stepped out first before reaching back to give her a hand. Her bags were already being grabbed by the driver, so she followed Cade into the house.

"Let me know if you have any issues with the contract. I would like to get that settled as soon as possible." Cade dropped her hand as they made it in the house.

"Sure," April answered. She waited for the driver to set her bags down and then picked them up and headed for the stairs.

"I didn't think to create an office space for you. I can clear some space in my office if you'd like to share. We can also use one of the spare rooms upstairs. Just let me know what you want to do, and I'll make sure it gets done."

She nearly laughed at him. He'd been in her apartment, she didn't have one there, wasn't worried about it now. "I'm good. I may post up in your living room sometimes, though."

"Whatever you need," he told her. He looked like he wanted to say something, but shook his head instead. "I'll see you in the morning unless you need anything?"

April shook her head. "I'm pretty tired, actually. I'll look over your contract and then probably go to sleep."

They went their separate ways. The awkwardness of that conversation stuck with her as she reviewed the contract. It was weird that after all they'd done, getting married, sleeping together, not to mention their past, that something as simple as good night was that uncomfortable.

The contract was very generous in her favor. Nothing was out of order aside from that and he'd even added a clause should one of them not be able to have children that put no fault on her. It wasn't something she'd considered, but now that she saw it there she was glad that he had.

She signed it and set it on her side table before laying back on the bed. Flipping on the TV, she ignored the work she'd brought home and let herself zone out, only thinking of Cade a few times.

Chapter Eighteen
Cade

Cade and April had settled into a sort of strange routine. It was a bit like living with a stranger but they made it work. Breakfast was usually had together and they took turns making things on the weekend, during the week she seemed to exist on tiny amounts of food.

It was Saturday and Cade had gotten up early, pulling together a big breakfast for the two of them. Bacon was cooked, he was flipping the last pancake and the eggs were ready to go in the pan. Having a cook was never his style and he'd been happy that April hadn't requested one, not that he thought she would.

April had been quieter than normal this week and barely eaten before work. Dinner hadn't been something they'd shared since right after they'd moved in, but he noticed little was gone from the fridge. If she was ordering food then she wasn't eating it here because he hadn't seen any takeout trash.

This morning he planned to remind her, again, that this was her home now too and she was welcome to anything. He didn't have a cook but he did have a driver and a few people that shopped for him.

Anything she wanted he was more than happy to get for her but she hadn't asked for anything.

She worked a lot. That was one of the first things he noticed and he hated it. He wanted her to cut back on her hours and take better care of herself, but knew he had no right to say those things to her. Still, maybe little by little he could convince her his idea was better, starting with a big breakfast this morning.

It felt like she was avoiding him and had been since their flight back from Vegas. He needed to fix that but didn't know where to start. He was also still deal with looking for his father which was turning out to be a waste of his time.

The man called several times a week, Cade didn't answer. Then his father would send a text and Cade would ignore that too. No one had been able to find out where he was sending it from, the encryption too thorough.

It was odd. They worked in technology but hiding things wasn't what they did in their company. Though, his father may have made contacts, he found it hard to believe that someone would help him like they were. Then, most people had a price and his father clearly had money stashed somewhere.

Usually, April was up just as early as him but he hadn't seen her yet. He wasn't going to hold sleeping in against her, but it seemed out of character for her. As he fixed the last of the eggs, he made up his mind that he would check on her if she didn't come down before they were done.

"Morning," April said, walking in the kitchen.

He turned to face her and watched as she took in the food on the counter. In the next second, she threw her hand over her mouth and ran away.

Cade set the eggs down and turned off the stove as he debated what to do. It seemed like anything nice he did for her was making her upset, including being near him. There could be only one reason for that, maybe she was in on things with his father.

It didn't make sense and she had no reason to work with him.

Nothing she could get out of it that he could quickly puzzle together other than more money. Hadn't he just been thinking that everyone had a price? It seemed that maybe someone had found hers.

Cade went in search of her, not wasting any more time thinking about it. She had shut herself in her bathroom. He knocked on the door, waiting for a response.

"April?" he called out when she didn't answer. "If you've done something that I need to know about just tell me."

He wasn't going to make fake promises not to be mad, but he needed to know. Only silence greeted him from the other side of the door. Knocking again, Cade stared at the handle and debated his next move.

Leaving her some privacy still, Cade backed away from the door and sat in the chair on the corner of her room. He would just wait her out, no matter that his knee was now bounding and he was only coming up with worse scenarios.

After five minutes and she still hadn't emerged, Cade went back to the door and knocked again. "April. We need to talk now, come out or I'm going to open this door." Not wanting to really do that, he continued. "If you're working with my father you need to just tell me what is going on. I can't have you here if you are keeping things from me and it will void our contract."

It wouldn't actually, and she would know that better than anyone. He hadn't thought to include anything about that in there. It was a shortsighted moment on his part that he was regretting now.

"April, just admit it and we can talk. Help me understand." He waited, still no response from her. He was beginning to wonder if he was talking to an empty room.

He didn't know if it was locked or not but he was about to find out. Putting his hand on the handle, he was surprised when it gave immediately. Pushing it open, he stepped into the bathroom.

What he hadn't expected was the water running in the sink, drowning out the sounds. He turned it off and looked for April.

Curled in the floor by the toilet, she moaned but didn't make an effort to move.

"Fuck," he said as he went to her.

There he had been on the other side of the door accusing her of working with his father and she was in here sick. He been an idiot and should have thought of that first. It made sense with the way she'd been acting.

"April, baby, are you okay?" He reached down and touched her forehead. Not warm, but clammy.

She groaned again but didn't open her eyes. Without another thought, he scooped her up, into his arms, holding her close as he took her out of the bathroom. Skipping past her bed, he carried her out of her room and put her where he wanted her, his bed.

"I've got you," he whispered to her as he lowered her down into his bed.

He felt her body lurch and ran to his own bathroom to get the trashcan to sit by the bed for her before crawling next to her. He rubbed small circles on her back until he felt her breathing even out and he knew she'd fallen back asleep.

Laying there next to her, Cade beat himself up, hoping that she hadn't heard all that he'd accused her of while she was just sick. He was a top-notch idiot and had a lot to do to make up for it.

While she slept, Cade finally rose and went to clean up from breakfast. He scarfed down some for himself and put the dishes in the sink, setting her plate in the microwave in case she felt better when she woke up. He also ordered some chicken soup in case she didn't.

As quickly as he could, he returned to her side. She was still sleeping and hadn't moved an inch. He checked her head again, but she didn't feel like she was running a fever. The good news was she felt less clammy.

He settled in next to her, pulling the covers around them both and held her lightly. He didn't move her and was careful not to disturb her. He ran his hand up and down her back, whispering soothing words to her all while hoping she didn't wake and get sick again.

"Cade?" she finally spoke.

"I'm here," he answered.

"I don't feel good." Her voice was weak.

"I know, baby. It's okay. I won't leave you." He wouldn't either. Thankfully it was the weekend so he didn't have anything to move or cancel which would take him from her side to get done. "Just rest."

"I think... I think I might be pregnant," she said.

Idiot. He was an idiot again. Why hadn't he considered that? "What do you need?" he asked.

"A test."

Cade jumped out of bed, quickly getting dressed for the day. "Is there a kind I should get?" he asked her.

"I don't know," she said, sitting up. "I've never done this before."

"No, of course you haven't. I'll just get all of them," he assured her.

April laughed. It was weak, but it was a laugh. "Just get a few."

"Anything else? I put a trashcan by the bed there."

She looked over at it. "Thank you. Nothing else that I can think of."

Cade went to her, pressing a kiss to her forehead. "Stay here. I'll be right back."

He nearly tripped trying to put his shoes on in his hurry to get out the door. He could send someone to do this but it would take longer. Besides, it felt too personal to send anyone else. Grabbing his keys, he was gone as every possible outcome rushed through his head.

The one thing he was sure of was that he wanted her to have his baby and it had nothing to do with his father.

Chapter Nineteen
April

April looked around Cade's room from her vantage point on his bed. Unsure how she got here, she felt out of place in Cade's darkly decorated room, so opposite to the light grey room she'd been given.

It suited him. That much was true, but she wasn't meant to be in here. The last thing she remembered was coming down for breakfast and the smell of bacon smacking her in the face. Then her stomach had turned against her and she'd made a run for her bathroom.

She'd gotten up once, thinking she was done, but then it had revolted again. Cade wasn't there, and she hadn't been sure enough herself to tell him her suspicions. They'd only slept together the one time, after all.

Her plan had been to get a test today, then she'd tell him if it was positive. No one knew what was going on, though it had been hard to hide at work. Every single smell was making her ill, and she was exhausted. Food was hard to keep down in the times she was able to eat, but she was trying her best to get some things in.

The front door slammed, making her jump. She heard the plastic bag as Cade ran up the stairs, stopping at the bedroom door. He was out of breath and she bit back a smile to see him so uncharacteristically disheveled. It was nice to know he was human, too.

"I got all the different kinds, but the lady at the register said this one was best." He held up a pink box.

"I'll do that one then." She moved the blankets and went to stand, only to find Cade right there at her side, helping her up. "I'll be right back," she told him, taking the box of tests.

It took a minute to get the package open and then read through the instructions. Easy enough, she peed on the stick and put the cap back on before opening the door. He was there on the other side, waiting.

"It says we have to wait three minutes. Can you start a timer?" She had no idea where her phone was.

He did, and she noticed his hands shook slightly. Reaching out to him, she took his free hand and squeezed it in her own.

"We'll know soon," she assured him. He was hard to read, and she didn't know which way he wanted this to go.

He nodded. "Two minutes," he laughed, holding his phone.

Neither of them left the bathroom doorway as they waited for the timer to go off. They stood there, both anxiously anticipating the results.

The quiet was so heavy over them that when his timer did go off, April jumped, startled.

"Do you want to go see?" Cade asked.

"Together," she said.

April still held his hand and hadn't noticed until she went to step back into the bathroom. He came with her, squeezing her hand as they did.

Looking down on the counter, the test was undeniable. Pregnant, the screen read. She looked in the mirror and watched Cade's reaction. A rare unguarded moment for him. She saw him smile before going back to his business face.

"We did it," Cade said.

"Sure did," April nodded, dropping his hand. "Now what?"

"I don't know. This is faster than I thought it would happen."

"That's for sure," she muttered. "We need to find a doctor."

"Yes. They can give you something so you won't be so sick." Cade began typing on his phone again.

"I don't think that's how it works. It's just morning sickness and it should go away."

He stopped typing and looked up at her. "When was the last time you ate?"

"Last night," she answered confidently.

"What did you eat?" he pressed.

He had her there. "Just some crackers. But I feel better right now."

"We need to find something you can eat. Is it just smelly things you don't like? Anything you think you might be able to eat?"

At the talk of food, her stomach clenched. She did her best to hide the sudden wave of nausea, but clearly not well enough. Cade lifted her off her feet and deposited her back into his bed.

"I'll see what I can find that you might be able to handle," he said before leaving the room.

April was yet again left alone with her thoughts. She had no idea how he felt about her being pregnant outside of the same shock that she was feeling. The small smile had given her hope, but it was fleeting.

Was he excited? She knew this was just a means to an end, but did he want the baby, really? She hadn't thought of that until now. Would he want to be around for the pregnancy?

Cade returned with a plate of cheese, crackers, and bananas. "I didn't know about the cheese, but I thought it was worth a try. We might need to get you a nurse to help with things."

A nurse? She was only pregnant, hardly worth of a private nurse. "Cade, calm down. It will be fine."

"You don't know that. We need you better or it's bad for the baby, that much I know. I don't know what the hell to do here." He sounded pissed, and she was confused.

Whether it was hormones or just the pent-up feelings since their wedding, she didn't know, but something set her off and it all rushed out.

"I don't need to be here anymore, I guess. I can just go back to my apartment until we see if I've fulfilled my end of the deal. Then you don't have to worry about it. I'll just let you know how the appointments go when I find a doctor."

"Is that what you want?" he asked.

"I don't know what I want!" she shouted. "I want to feel better and I want the baby to be okay. I want to know how all of this is supposed to work because I thought I understood things, but I really don't."

"What is that supposed to mean?"

"Exactly what I said. I won't be confined to be by you because my stomach is upset." Cade opened his mouth, and she held up a palm, stopping him. "If the doctor orders me to bed, then that's a different thing entirely. I'm stressed, confused, and so tired, Cade. I think I'm just going to go to bed."

Cade was shocked. He wasn't hiding it, and it was just as well because she was, too.

"Sorry. I just don't know what to do," she admitted. "I'm scared."

He looked at her but didn't speak right away. "I'll leave you to it, then. Let me know if there's anything either of you need. I want to be at the appointments."

April nodded. "You aren't going to take the baby from me, are you?" she whispered.

"Take the baby? What the fuck? Have I given you any reason to think I would do that?" Cade didn't shout, but she could tell he wanted to rage at her.

She shook her head.

"Sleep wherever. Let me know if you need anything." Cade turned and stormed out of his room.

She stood there feeling like she'd ruined everything before leaving the room, too. Back in her own bedroom, she curled up in the bed and let the tears out. Fear was driving everything now, and she didn't even fully know what all she was scared of.

The unknown was looming over her, waiting to pull the rug out from under her feet and laugh. She let the exhaustion wash over her and slept instead of thinking about it. She'd sort it out later, when she felt better.

Chapter Twenty
Cade

Cade sighed as he sat at his kitchen table, alone. He and April had been on edge with each other and everyone since Saturday. She went back to work yesterday, but he'd taken off early to get home closer to when she did.

She looked exhausted, and he wanted to comfort her but couldn't bring himself to do it. April thought he was going to take the child from her, and it made him feel like shit. Why she would think that he wanted to claim he didn't know, but he understood it the fear attached to everything.

Sunday, they hadn't spoken much and Monday, he'd asked her about the doctor, but she hadn't made an appointment. Then she'd looked miserable, so he hadn't pressed it, but now he was waiting on her to come down to press the issue.

An appointment needed to be made so they could check out not only the baby, but her as well. He hated seeing her be sick, and she only looked like she felt worse and worse with each passing day. A doctor would be able to help her with the nausea and then maybe he could move towards working on their relationship instead.

Cade had been careful not to make or bring any food into the house, deciding that April could tell him what she would or could eat tonight. He was hungry, but he pushed that aside, waiting to see what she would want first.

"Hey," he stood from the table as she joined him in the kitchen.

"Hey." That was it, one word.

"Were you able to make an appointment today?"

April shook her head. "I have it on my list for tomorrow, but I've had no time today. I promise it's nothing too crazy to make one now. Everything I read said doctors don't normally see the mothers until they are eight weeks along, and I'm not quite there yet."

"I know, but I think it would help you to maybe be able to eat," he pressed.

"I'm trying, Cade," she said. "I have a lot going on, but I will take care of the baby."

Cade reached out and touched her arm, trying to soothe her. "I'm not worried about the baby as much as I'm worried about you."

To his surprise, she didn't pull away from his touch, and he felt her lean towards him ever so slightly. "Thank you."

She stepped away then and went to the fridge. She pulled out a small bowl of leftover rice, putting it in the microwave.

Silence loomed heavy in the air as the microwave hummed. He waited for her to grab her food and return to the table before sitting down and joining her. After she ate and was settled down for the night, he'd go out and eat something.

There was no way he was going to bring food into the house, knowing she'd likely get sick again. If the rice stayed down, then at least it was something.

"How about if I make the appointment?" he offered.

"I can do it," she said.

"I know. I never said that you couldn't, but I think I am more worried about you than you are at this point. I just want to make sure you're okay. You can't survive on rice forever, even if this only lasts a few more weeks."

She stopped eating and looked up at him. He saw it before she moved. The rice didn't sit well with her either.

April pushed the food away and ran from the table. Cade was hot on her heels as she made it to the downstairs bathroom and lost the little bit of dinner she'd been able to eat.

"This isn't safe, baby," he whispered, rubbing her back. "We have to get you better."

Right now, he didn't care about the baby as much as her. There would be other chances, other ways that made her less sick if that's what it took. He just needed her to be okay.

"Sorry," she said as she backed away from the toilet. "You didn't need to follow me."

"Of course, I didn't need to. Let me take care of you, April," he pleaded.

When she didn't answer, Cade decided to press his luck tonight and pick her up. One small cry of shock was all she gave before wrapping her arms around him.

He considered what to do next as he carried her up the stairs. His own thoughts were running a million miles a second. Making a decision as he hit the top of the stairs, he turned into his bedroom. There was nowhere else he wanted her, and he needed her there in his bed.

She gave him a questioning look, but didn't argue. Instead, she settled into the bed and curled into the covers.

It seemed that dinner wasn't on the docket for tonight. He needed to work on his own thoughts and feelings, deciding what he actually wanted with April. After that, he'd had to come up with a way to make sure she wanted the same thing.

Quickly, he moved around the room and got himself ready for bed before sliding in next to her. "Is this okay?" he asked as he dropped one arm around her middle, holding her loosely.

"Yes," she said, sounding already close to sleeping.

Cade lay there and let his thoughts drift over everything that was to come. If they stuck with the contract, how things could play out, and what could happen if they didn't?

He wanted her. That much was clearer to him now than it ever had been, not just in his bed, but in his life. He wanted her as a partner and to be there with him for everything that was still to come.

It was not as much of a shock as he had thought it would be, nor was it hard to sort his feelings. If he were to practice total honesty, he would have to admit that it was what he wanted all along. The reason he'd pursued her and only her after his father's ridiculous demand.

Back to thinking of his father. He needed to find a way that kept her from any of the fallout from what could happen there. It was foolish of him to think that he could just outsmart his father and he would let it go. He'd only dragged her into his giant mess.

Tomorrow he'd have to make her an appointment, get her feeling better, and then tell her what he wanted. Honesty was going to go the furthest with April, and he would just lay it all out for her and see where it went.

Surprisingly, he felt calm as he thought about it. He had expected more of a panic over the thoughts about her and coming to terms with his feelings. This was going to change a lot in his life, but he felt at ease with every change that crossed his mind.

He wanted to come home to her every night and to have a few kids with her. There was no concern about April being a mother. He knew she would be great at it and nothing like his own parents. Their kids would be loved and they would know it.

As he continued to think about it, he convinced himself that April felt the same way. Everything that had happened between them on their wedding day told him that April was, at the very least, interested in him, but he thought it was more.

Settled, Cade held her close and listened to her even breathing. It was all going to be okay somehow, and this would just be the beginning of better things to come. Even his father's threats didn't matter as long as April was here with him, safe.

Chapter Twenty-One
April

By Saturday night, April was more confused than ever. Cade had taken her to a doctor appointment on Wednesday and had pressed the poor doctor until they had conceded that maybe she needed some medicine and had given her something for the nausea. He asked very few questions about the baby and was focused entirely on her.

It made her feel so cared for, but she couldn't help but remind herself constantly that this was a contract. Did it matter that she was now sleeping in his bed every night? Did it matter that the words he was saying were perfect and made her feel loved? No. This was a contract between them, a means to an end with a baby in the middle of it.

For that, she felt awful. It was fine when the baby was fictional, or at least not real yet. Now that there was an actual life growing inside of her, she felt terrible that it wouldn't have two parents and it was arranged to be that way. What kind of mother was she to give into her own wild desires for this man and make a baby into this nonsense?

"You ready?" Cade interrupted her self-deprecating inner monologue.

They were having the whole friend group over to announce her pregnancy and no, she wasn't ready. "Sure," she said without much cheer behind it.

"April." Cade crouched down in front of her at the vanity where she was getting ready. "You know we don't have to do this, right? I can cancel everything and tell them via text."

She sighed. "It's fine. I like everyone, so I'm sure it will go well."

He gave her a look that screamed he didn't believe her. "This might not be the right time, but I think I need to do this anyway. I wanted to wait until you were feeling better, but then with work and everything, we've been a little busy the last two days."

April's mind raced with every negative thing that he could be getting ready to tell her. One thing she knew for certain about this man was that he didn't ramble, ever. If she were to tell anyone that he was right now, they'd call her a liar and she wouldn't blame them.

"I want to make this real. I want to tear up the contract and I want you in my bed every night from now until forever."

Her mouth fell open. There were no words that would have done what she felt any justice and her brain wasn't working to form any, anyway.

Cade rose up and kissed her forehead. "Just think about it for me?"

The doorbell rang and with another chaste kiss, he walked out of their now shared bedroom and left her sitting there, shocked. She didn't follow him immediately, needing time to recover even if she couldn't process what he had said.

"Cade said it was okay to come up?" Kayla knocked as she came into the room.

April closed her mouth and turned back to the mirror to finish her makeup. "You're fine. Just finishing up getting ready."

"Wow," Kayla said, looking around as she came in. "This is so very Cade."

She laughed. That had also been her first thought. "Isn't it? That's what I thought at first, too. I think it's growing on me, though."

"I bet it is," Kayla laughed with a wink.

"If I changed it, he would look so out of place in here," April told her.

"Oh absolutely. I think I vase with some pretty flowers would brighten things up though and I'm positive this is new." She pointed at the vanity.

Kayla laughed with her. It was good to be around her friend again. Maybe that was what she needed to really let go of everything tonight and just enjoy her friends.

"Ready?" Kayla asked.

April nodded. They walked downstairs together, finding that most of their group had already arrived. They were waiting on Jake and Lauren still, but everyone else was here except for Owen and Jessica, who weren't able to make it.

Cade sought her out the moment they entered the living room. He was right there at her side, one hand on the small of her back as it always was and the other one passing her a plate of food.

Since the doctor had helped with the nausea for now, Cade had been feeding her at every opportunity. She didn't have the heart to tell him to stop just yet, but if she kept eating like this, he was going to have to roll her out the front door.

"Wine?" Kayla offered her a glass.

"None for me tonight, thank you," April waved her off.

Kayla didn't stop staring at her. Her friendly gaze turned questioning before her eyes lit up. "Are you?" She made a rounded motion at her stomach.

"I'm going to need you to stop being so perceptive and give us a chance to make our own announcement," Cade joked.

"Shut up!" Kayla squealed.

"Oh, please don't shut up. I want to know, too," Lauren joined them.

"I didn't see you guys come in," Cade said before turning to April. "Should we just do it now?"

April smiled back at him and nodded.

"Everyone!" he shouted to get their attention. "April and I have an announcement to make." Cade looked down at her and smiled. "We're expecting!"

Cheers came from everyone.

Catherine pushed past all the guys to hug them both. "I'm going to be an aunt! This is so exciting!"

April looked around to see all their friends were excited for them. Evan Ryker was smiling, and that was a rare occasion from what little she knew of the man. Everyone, that is, except Luke, who was looking grumpy at the end of the sofa and not looking their way.

"Ignore him. He's still too young to understand that life isn't about sleeping around," Cade whispered.

Fair enough, she thought. Everyone knew Luke was a playboy and didn't want to settle down. Maybe he was just upset it was getting closer and closer to his own turn to date. Ryker was next, but it seemed no one was in a hurry to tell him that.

Catherine was stepping away, answering her phone, and she looked up to see Cade watching her.

"Can you believe it? You're going to be a grandma!" Catherine was squealing.

Leaving her side, Cade went to her and yanked her phone away. "Just because I told you doesn't mean that you get to go off spreading it around. If I wanted our elusive parents to know, then I would have told them."

"Cade!" Catherine shouted back. "They're our parents. You can't just pretend they don't exist and leave them out of everything."

"Fucking watch me."

Cade turned and left them all standing there, watching him walk out the front door. No one knew what had just happened except April, and even then, she was confused. The plan had been for her to get pregnant, so why wouldn't he want his parents to know?

"What is up with him?" Catherine asked April.

"I think it's just the stress of everything. I know he has plans of how to tell everyone, so maybe that was something he was going to do with just us?" That wasn't it, but it sounded like a good enough thing to say. She could only hope that anyone believed her.

"Cade doesn't normally get like that, except when it comes to his father. I'd just leave him be for now. He'll come back soon enough," Lauren told her, squeezing her shoulders.

"Yeah. Everyone eat up. We bought all this food and Cade won't stop feeding me, so please eat it all before I do," she laughed.

The rest of the evening went okay. There was no more mention of Cade's outburst, but the mood was not what it was before. After about two hours, mostly everyone had left except Catherine.

"I feel bad that I ruined everything tonight," she told April.

"It's not your fault. You couldn't have known that was going to happen," April reassured her.

Catherine hung around for a little bit longer, helping her clean up and probably waiting for Cade to come back. In the end, she left April alone to think about what had just happened.

Cade returned a little bit later while she was dozing on the sofa. He said nothing at first, only came to her and knelt in front, resting his head next to hers.

"I'm sorry," he whispered.

April hadn't been mad. She knew the relationship between him and his parents, so she'd been more concerned than anything.

"Don't apologize. Tell me what's going on." She ran her fingers through his hair as she waited for him to reply.

"He demanded that I annul our wedding and if I didn't, he was going to cause more trouble. I don't understand what he wants and why he keeps doing this. I think he's losing his mind and I can't find him." He collapsed beside her, and April knew what it took to admit everything. It was a list a defeat for him, something he didn't take lightly.

"You need to tell her," April told him, still running her nails over his scalp.

"I don't want to ruin things between them. All of this seems directed at me for now, and I was trying to shield her from it."

April shifted to sit and look at him. "Your sister is a strong woman. It might hurt her some, but she's damn sure going to recover from it and get stronger in the process."

He was quiet for so long she thought he wasn't going to reply. When he stood, she thought he was going to walk away again, instead he bent down and picked her up.

"What are you doing?" she laughed.

"Putting you in bed where you belong."

"I can walk," she reminded him.

"Yeah, but you don't have to."

He kissed her lips before heading to the bedroom. Nothing else was said about what was going on with Catherine and his parents. She let it drop. It didn't need to be decided tonight.

Chapter Twenty-Two
Cade

Cade took a deep breath as he waited for Catherine to answer her door. April was right, and he needed to at least tell his sister what was going on. The problem was, he didn't know if she'd believe him.

"Hey," she answered the door, pulling it wide for him to come in.

"Hey," he said back, unsure where to start.

"Have a seat. I'll be right back," she turned toward her room.

It only then occurred to him that he probably should have called first. "You don't, umm, have someone here, do you? I can leave and come back. I should have called first." Cade started for the door.

"Cade stop. There's no one here. I'm just going to brush my teeth." Catherine laughed as she left him standing there, feeling like an idiot again.

It was terrible enough that he'd come home and dumped everything on April after abandoning her earlier in the night. Now he'd made a fool out of himself in front of his sister, one she'd likely never let him forget.

"Okay. I feel better now. What are you doing here?" Catherine came back into her living room.

Cade was still standing there. "I have something to tell you."

"I figured as much. Just spit it out. I can't help if you don't tell me what's going on and frankly, you're scaring me right now."

He thought it over for half a second before just letting the words out. "Our parents are behind all the bad things that are happening to the restaurant. Well, Father is, I don't know Mother's role specifically, but she's helping him for sure."

Catherine laughed. "What?"

"I'm serious." He finally took a seat on her sofa and turned to face her. "Father has been threatening me for a while now and I haven't told anyone. When I try to find him, it's useless. I don't know where he's getting help, but it's damn good."

"Ryker has a guy—"

"I know. No luck."

"What do you mean, he's been threatening you?"

Cade sighed. Here came the part he was dreading. "Most recently, he was mad that I want on my blind date. Then demanded that I get married and produce an heir."

Catherine looked at him like he's lost his mind, and maybe he had.

"It doesn't make any sense, but he threatened to do more to the restaurant and to everyone if I didn't. Then he said he'd pull you into it and I didn't want that to happen. So I talked April into marrying me and, well, we got her pregnant faster than expected. But I don't want to lose her, Cat. I just am so tired of dealing with this shit."

"That's why you've been asking where they were?" she still sounded like she didn't believe him.

"Yes. I know he was the one putting Lauren's mother up to things. Well, maybe not putting her up to it, but he was financing it. She was capable of the nonsense havoc she created all on her own." He stood and started pacing. "Think about it. The one thing we've wondered with Lauren's mom is how she was able to hire anyone."

"Right. That doesn't mean it was Father. And what the hell? Produce an heir? Are we in a historical romance novel now?" She looked around. "If we are, then it's not well done. The TV is kind of modern."

"I'm not joking. I'm really fucking not. I wish I was." God, did he wish he was.

"So you're wanting me to believe that Father is behind all the problems that have been happening lately? And that no one can find an old white man with a lot of money hiding somewhere?"

"That's exactly what I'm saying. He found out I married April somehow without me telling him and before the article in the paper. I'm still not really sure how, though I wasn't exactly super quiet with it at her work." It was still bothering him because it felt like there was a spy in their midst. "He demanded I annul it because she wasn't who he wanted me to marry. Threatened something else would happen and then it did."

"Cade, sit down. You're making me nervous with all that pacing."

He did, but they both knew it wouldn't last long. "The fire outside the restaurant was just after he threatened it. It's not a coincidence, Cat. I know that you don't want to believe me, but it's all true. I don't know what he's going to do now that he knows she's expecting and I'm really not going to end the marriage. I don't want to."

She was quiet for a moment, processing, he guessed. "First, I'm glad you don't want to end things with her."

"We have a contract. I wasn't kidding. Now I need to make her believe that I don't want it anymore while keeping Father from her."

"Let's talk this over. Do you have anything you can show me for proof?"

Cade handed over his phone. There wasn't much in their messages beck and forth, but a few veiled threats. Catherine was smart enough to pick up on them, though.

"This doesn't show much. I agree he's threatening you, but—" She was interrupted by someone at the door.

"Are you expecting anyone?" Cade asked.

Catherine shook her head. He went to the door to answer it and nearly fell out when he saw who was there.

"Just the two people I wanted to see!" His mother pushed past him and into Catherine's apartment.

"Mother," Cade greeted. "What are you doing here?"

"Your father wanted me to come and check on the two of you. He said that you had been up to no good lately and thought I might be able to talk some sense into you and keep Catherine from making the same foolish decisions."

The suitcase she was wheeling along had been set in the middle of the living room as she turned to Catherine, taking her in.

"Mother, I have plans. I won't just be around here to stay with you," Catherine tried, eyeing the suitcase.

"That's fine, dear. I don't need anything. Your maid and cook can help with whatever."

Catherine turned to Cade for help, her eyes pleading. Though both of them had been raised in homes with full staff, neither of them had any full time. They had shoppers, and that was it. Both preferring to have their homes to themselves.

"Catherine doesn't have staff," Cade reminded her.

"Well, she can get some now. I'm sure I'll be staying for a bit while you sort out your messes. You know you have your father very upset over your choices. Besides, just because you knock up a whore doesn't mean you need to marry her."

"Mother!" Both of them shouted at her.

"My wife is not a whore, or anything else. She is the woman that I am married to and just to stick to your points here, the baby came after."

"Yes dear. That's what everyone used to say. I think it's less taboo now to have a baby out of wedlock."

He was in the same bad novel as Catherine, and he hated it.

"What is Father planning to do if I don't leave her?" Cade asked.

"I don't know his plans. I know he has some. The both of you are really ungrateful considering the upbringing you had that taught you to be much better than this."

"He wouldn't hurt any of us, right?" Catherine asked.

She was starting to see the crazy for what it was and while he was happy he was no longer alone, he didn't want her to have to go through this. That was one of the main reasons he'd kept it from her and his friends.

"I don't know what his plans are, Catherine. I just told you that. Now, have you changed the bed since that other woman was staying here?" She changed the subject like it didn't matter if he was willing to hurt anyone.

"No." Catherine stood up. "I'm afraid that you'll need to get a hotel or something, because I have plans, as I said. I also have no staff, as you've been reminded. And I had no idea that you were coming. Where even have you been?"

She turned to Catherine with a glare. "I can see I've been too late in arriving. Your brother has clearly brainwashed you."

"Mother? Aren't you excited that Cade is having a baby? A grandchild for you to spoil?" Catherine said.

Cade kept quiet to see where she was going with this. He didn't really need the baby brought up again, but knew she must have had a plan.

"No. That baby is no grandchild of mine. My grandchildren will come from good stock and impeccable families. This is merely a hiccup." She waved Catherine off.

"I'm afraid you're going to have to leave now." Catherine pointed at the door. "I don't have time for this today and I'm sure you'd be much happier in a hotel. I will stand with my brother on this one and if you say anything bad about April or the baby, you can just stop reaching out to me as well. I don't want anything to do with someone who is so stuck up they can't be happy for their children."

Catherine pulled the door open wide and pointed out. Their mother looked between them before huffing and walking out the door. Catherine shut it with a firmness that screamed she would have slammed it if she could.

"Okay, let's say I believe you." She turned to him.

Chapter Twenty-Three
April

April was back at work and feeling renewed at her job. Not that she loved it again, but she definitely was back at it after feeling like crap for the last couple of weeks. With her stomach finally under control, her focus was amazing.

She had worked from home some yesterday to catch back up so her boss wouldn't be able to comment on the fact that she had missed time for being sick. Until she had the baby she needed this job to be able to save for what came next.

Yes, Cade said he was all in but she still wasn't about to just forget that she thought he was once before. That hadn't ended well for her. This time she was taking it with more caution.

He had confided in his sister what he thought his parents were up to, well his father. She had come by last night to talk about it more and brought baby things by. The kid was the size of a peanut and was already being spoiled.

This morning Cade had tried to get her to go to lunch with him today. Not wanting to rile her boss any more than necessary, she'd packed one instead and turned down his offer. She was going to have a working lunch today.

"Good morning, April," Tucker greeted her. "Any chance that marriage is over?"

April rolled her eyes at his blatant question. "I'm not ending my marriage and if I did I wouldn't be ready to date anyone."

"Well, you let me know if you change your mind. I'll keep some space open on my calendar," he offered.

"I promise that's not necessary. I really would appreciate if you stopped hitting on me." April sat straighter as she spoke, annoyed with him.

He walked off laughing. April couldn't quite figure it out. He'd hit on her before but between last week and this one he'd really stepped it up like her marriage was more of a turn-on. She wasn't interested. If he didn't quit she just might tell Cade about it and let him deal with the problem for her.

Before she could settle back into her next contract, Mark appeared at her desk. Annoyed with the interruptions, April gave him a tight smile and waited to see what he had to say.

"Can you join me in my office?" he asked.

Something was wrong. She knew it immediately. He was usually more friendly even if he had something bad to say. This was a problem and she racked her brain as she followed him into his office and he closed the door behind them.

She'd drawn a blank on anything that she may have done wrong other than miss some time last week, but she'd more than made up for it and was even ahead of her deadlines. Did a client complain?

"Have a seat, April. I have something that we need to discuss." Mark sat behind his desk, his bald head reflecting the overhead light.

"I'm sorry, did I do something wrong?" she asked, wanting to be put out of her own misery.

"I am actually doing you a favor. The partners want to speak to you today and you know I've been grooming you for the partnership."

April cringed. She hated that word, grooming, it sounded so wrong.

"We got some disturbing news overnight and wanted to give you a chance to tell your side of things."

"I really don't know what you mean." She twisted her hands in her lap wishing he would just come out with it already.

"We received information that you are expecting. I know it isn't like you to make big decisions like that without thinking it through. It would certainly impact your future here at the firm."

His phone rang and he stopped talking to answer it. She sat, reeling, and trying to decide how to even react to this information. It didn't matter to her if she didn't get partner, she didn't want it anyway but to have it snatched from her because she got pregnant was insane.

"We can head in to the conference room now," Mark told her as he hung up the phone.

"Okay." April stood and followed him again, still confused.

As she turned the corner, she could see all the partners through the glass walls of the conference room. She was really going to have to announce to everyone that she was pregnant right now.

Why was she even concerned? She didn't want to make partner, she reminded herself. It still hurt and she knew that she'd be treated differently because of not wanting it now.

She stepped into the conference room and took a deep breath. They asked her to sit and she took it, preparing to explain herself.

It took all of fifteen minutes before she was dismissed. They sent her home for the day and April didn't bother to take her computer. So much for catching up or working hard. None of it mattered now.

She called the car back to get her and managed to hold it together until she was home. As soon as the door closed behind her, she let the tears fall. Cade called and she answered the phone with a sniff.

"Are you okay?"

"Someone told my boss I'm pregnant," her words were full of tears, she knew he'd be able to tell.

"Where are you?" She heard him moving around.

"I'm home. You don't need to come home now. I'm just being

dramatic right now." She was. It was uneccesary for her to be this worked up over a job she didn't even want.

"Stay there. I'll be home in a minute."

"Okay," she didn't argue again.

Truth be told, she wanted him here with her. Wanted him to tell her it was all going to be okay even when neither of them could predict the future.

She pulled out her lunch and made herself comfortable in the living room before digging into her salad. It was satisfying to stab her fork into as her sadness and confusion moved to anger.

They had no right to question her being pregnant. Why had they done that? It wasn't like they could fire her over it. They couldn't even not offer her the partnership over it or she could sue them. They knew that, it was common knowledge and against the damn law.

"Hey, baby," Cade said as he walked in. "How are you doing?"

"Fine." Stab. "Just freaking fine." Another stab.

Cade laughed and reached for her bowl. "I don't think the salad deserves your anger."

"It was helping," she shrugged and let him take it.

"I'm glad that it was. You aren't crying anymore, so I'll thank the salad for it and then save it from further harm."

April couldn't help but laugh. "I don't understand what happened today. I've been trying to think it over, but it doesn't make sense. They can't actually fire me for it."

"No, but it's an at-will state so they can fire you for no reason. They could even call it downsizing or position elimination." Cade explained. "We could still sue them for it because it's obvious why, but they would have that argument."

"I think they wanted me to lie. I think they were looking for me to lie about so they could ignore it or maybe fire me for lying."

The more she thought about it the more angry she got. She wanted to know how they knew but that was unliklely.

"Come on. Let's do anything else. How about a movie? I'll even let you pick something terrible," Cade teased.

"Oh, is that a challenge? I can do a really bad one." Happy not to dwell on the fact that her life was falling apart, or her career was anyway, she played back.

"I remember you used to be really bad at choosing movies," he told her.

"Just because you don't like it doesn't mean it's bad." She snatched the remote. "Maybe something with subtitles?"

She laughed as Cade tackled her, pretending to try to take the remote. He was careful to keep his weight off her but she was just so happy he was here for her that she didn't want it to end.

"I could put on a documentary," Cade joked.

"No way! This is for entertainment, not learning."

"I am entertained when I learn," he laughed and backed away. "I'll go make us some popcorn."

"I want to learn about how this guy and girl get together," she yelled back toward him before picking a romance and waiting for him to return.

She knew Cade would sit here and watch it from start to finish. He always did even when he didn't like the movie. She used to wonder if he secretly liked the romance movies and her picking them just gave him an excuse to watch them. Then after it was over he'd complain for an hour about what was so bad about the movie.

Cade came back with two large bowls of popcorn and handed her one. Then he grabbed one large blanket and wrapped it around them both before sitting next to her and draping one arm around her shoulders, keeping her close.

Another time she'd explain about the partnership and the full extent of the impromptu meeting she'd been pulled into, but right now, she was going to forget it all and rest her head on Cade. She'd pretend everything was right in the world because when she was sitting here like this with him it was.

Chapter Twenty-Four
Cade

Cade hadn't let go of the fact that April's bosses had hurt her. By Wednesday morning, he had decided that it must have been his father and had called a meeting with his friends. They were due in his office at any minute.

Today was about confessions, and he was prepared to tell everyone what was going on. No more hiding it, not taking it all on himself. April had told him last night as they laid in the bed that he needed to share the burden and let others help.

She'd told him that just because he could do it alone didn't mean he had to. It wasn't anything he didn't already know, of course, but hearing her say it had made it click for him. His friends wouldn't judge him, he knew that they'd help.

"What's going on?" Jake walked in, taking a seat.

"I'd rather just explain it once," Cade answered.

"Okay, fine," Jake pretended to pout.

Cade was surprised that Lauren hadn't followed Jake in as she usually did. They must have both understood that Cade needed this to be just between them.

One by one, his friends showed up. Luke last, as always. As they took their seats, Cade stood and closed the door, shutting them in. It gave him a moment to remind himself that they would understand.

"I need to tell you all something and I need your help," he addressed the group.

It took him nearly ten minutes to fully explain everything to his friends. He left nothing out, including the fact that he was pretty sure his father had been the one to tell April's work that she was pregnant. She didn't need that job anyway, but he didn't like seeing her upset.

"What the fuck?" Jake was the first to speak. "I always hated your father, but I think he's off his rocker."

"Definitely could use a mental evaluation," Evan agreed. "Does dementia run in your family?"

Cade shrugged. He didn't know, but he hoped not.

"You knew this whole time who was behind all of this and didn't think to tell any of us?" Luke demanded.

"Knock it off," Ryker told him.

"No. I'm not going to knock it off. You put them through a lot of shit because you didn't want to tell us and now you want us to help you?"

"What is wrong with you?" Evan asked, just as shocked as Cade as the outburst.

"What is wrong with you?" Luke countered. "You're just going to sit here and take this shit? He's been lying to us!"

Luke stood and stormed out, slamming the door when he did. Cade looked around and everyone else who appeared just as lost as he was.

"We can deal with that shit later," Ryler finally said. "I'm not unpacking a bunch of feelings because the kid is acting like a fucking idiot."

"Awe, no one asked about your feelings, big guy," Cade teased.

Ryker grunted and everyone laughed.

"Okay, back to business. What can we do to help?" Evan asked.

"I don't even know. I am all up for ideas or anything you think that might help me find him or get him to stop this shit."

"I have a guy that does this kind of thing," Ryker said.

Cade bit back a smile. "I know. He hasn't found him yet either."

"What the fuck. Y'all know I'm the one paying him, right? And it's not to do any of your and your sister's shit."

"I can't speak for her, but it was more of a side job. I was paying him," Cade said, knowing it wouldn't make Ryker feel any better about the situation.

"At this point, I think he's community property," Evan added. "I've hired him too."

"What the fuck?" Cade growled. "Get your own employees."

"Awe, but you have the best one for that stuff," Jake pretended to pout.

The room broke out into laughter at Ryker's face. After a few minutes, they mostly had themselves under control and returned to the reason they were all here.

The conversation went better than Cade had expected, and they called Lauren in for perspective. It took a few minutes to catch her up and then ask for her opinion.

"When my mom does these things, it's all motivated by money. I don't think I'd be much help in sorting out your father, unfortunately. Can I say now that I never liked him?" Lauren made a face.

"Maybe we need to find out who else would need the money enough to do these things for him?" Jake said.

It was as good a place as any to start. The problem was that there were too many options if they worked that way. The amount of money that everyone in the room had at their disposal meant that pretty much everyone was a suspect.

They discussed it for a while and always came back to the same result, nothing. The options were too broad or non-existent.

"You said your mother is in town?" Ryker asked.

"Showed up right after Catherine told her about the baby," Cade confirmed.

"Have Catherine meet with her somewhere and see what she can find out. Maybe if she can go to her hotel room, she can find anything out about her itinerary," Ryker said.

"I really don't have to involve her like that if we can avoid it. Maybe I should try first. Take her to dinner and see if she lets something slip."

"It's a solid plan," Jake agreed.

Cade sent a text off to his mother and then focused back on the conversation.

"I still feel like we have to be missing something here. Sure there's the outdated notion of heirs and whatnot, but this is coming from somewhere, some trigger," Evan mused.

"Like me banning him from the company?" Cade suggested. It was what he had assumed started it all.

"But he was acting stranger than normal before then. All the things he said about me and Lauren, for one. Things had been escalating slowly before then because it's what drove you to make that decision," Jake reminded him.

"Agreed. I think we need to look back further for something that might have happened," Evan said.

Ryker stood and paced for a moment before speaking. "Is there anything in his past that would make him think there is a different heir if something happened to you? Someone that isn't Catherine?"

Cade shook his head. "Nothing that I know of, but my parents don't exactly talk often and wouldn't talk about skeletons in their closets." It was a solid lead. He didn't know how to dig it up, but it made sense.

"Press that angle delicately when you talk to your mother. It might give you something. In the meantime, I'll have MY employee see what he can dig up." Ryker made for the door. "From now on, I want any consulting run by me first."

They all laughed. It was no secret among them that everyone had tapped his shoulder at some point except from Ryker, apparently. The fact that it bothered him this much was a guarantee that the man would never be short on work from the rest of them without talking to Ryker first.

"You're all a bunch of assholes," Ryker muttered before letting himself out.

"What about the woman I replaced?" Lauren asked. "She might know something, though I don't know if she'd be willing to spill any of it."

"Now that Ryker is gone too, I think we also need to talk about what is going on with Luke," Evan said.

"I think we deal with one problem at a time. Luke will come around. He's just being his usual self when things don't go his way," Cade said. It was bothering him about Luke, but he couldn't split his focus and this was more pressing. He genuinely hoped he grew up sooner rather than later because he was starting to get on Cade's nerves.

"Set up dinner and let's see what happens from there." Jake stood, taking Lauren's hand.

"We can let Ryker deal with Luke for now, but I think it's important enough that we all need to have a chat very soon." Evan looked worried. "Also, I assume I can tell Kayla what's going on?"

Cade nodded. "In private please? I don't want it getting out that he's behaving like this unless I have to. Even then, that's a Catherine thing."

"Agreed," Evan frowned. "I'm also concerned that there's someone that's telling him what's going on even if by accident."

"None of it makes sense, though. Who would do that and why?"

"Back to the original questions. We'll just have to wait and see what happens next. Maybe with a lead on where the money is coming from, we will have more ammunition for an interrogation," Jake said.

"I can go visit my mother and see what she has to say about things. Now that we know where the money is coming from, we might get something from her," Lauren offered.

Cade sighed. It was a good idea, but he didn't want her to be in harm's way.

"Let's hold off on that for now. We can save it for later if we need to, but I don't want you going to visit her if you don't have to."

Lauren nodded, but didn't look like she agreed.

"I'll keep an eye on her," Jake assured him, catching Cade's eye.

"I also think we should exclude Luke from these plans for now," Evan said.

"What are you thinking?" Cade recognized that look of suspicion.

"Nothing I'm ready to share yet. I have a new task for Ryker's employee, though," he laughed.

Chapter Twenty-Five
April

April was annoyed again. After Cade's confession that he wanted things to be real between them, he'd backed away. She knew he was dealing with things with his father, but it felt personal, and she didn't know where she stood again.

Then there was the work issue. She'd come back to work the next day after the conversation with the partners and everyone acted like nothing happened except she was getting contracts taken from her with no explanation.

This past weekend had been miserable as she tried to sort out what Cade was thinking and what was happening at work. It was Monday now, and she'd come up with nothing for answers. Mark was blatantly ignoring her today and Cade wasn't as blatant about it, but he wasn't really talking to her, either.

She needed a vacation from all the drama in her life. Everything before her date with Cade had been going okay, and now it was a mess. Sure, she wanted a new job before then, but the one she had wasn't at risk then.

"April," Mark said.

She jumped, fully immersed in her thoughts. She hadn't noticed him walk up. "Sorry. You scared me." She pressed a hand to heart to still the racing. "How can I help you?"

"If you can join me in my office, please?" He didn't wait for her, just walked away.

"Okay then." April stood and made her way across the office to his open door, closing it behind her. This was sure to be something that no one else should hear.

"Please have a seat."

She did, but sighed. "No offense Mark, but if you have something to say, I'd really prefer that you just got to it." Something had to give in her life and if this was it, then so be it.

"Yes, well. We have noticed that your work has been slipping lately and would like to sever our relationship with you and the firm."

April couldn't even pretend to be shocked. "What are you offering me?" she asked. Surely there was some type of severance at play here.

Mark slid her a document. She scanned through it. Less than three months' salary for all the ears she'd put into this firm? Fine. She didn't want to be here, anyway.

"Pen?" She held her hand out for him to give her one. "Just so I'm clear on this. You want everything to be effective immediately and are removing my non-complete clause?" April knew what it said, but she needed to make sure Mark did.

He winced. "This isn't my decision, April. I did fight to have that non-compete moved and I hope that you are able to find another position. We both know that you won't have the same time after the baby is born, anyway."

"I didn't do anything wrong here. Nothing. I don't need your sympathy, Mark. What you're pulling is illegal, but I don't want to be here anymore either."

She signed the paper and left it sitting on his desk before walking out. There was nothing left for her to say.

Choking back a bubble of laughter as she turned the corner to see her desk being packed, she struggled for calm. She snatched her phone off her desk and called for the car to come pick her up.

"Since you seem so capable, you can all carry those down for me." She didn't know where this show of strength was coming from, but she was going to ride high on it while she had it. She didn't give a flip what was in those boxes anymore. Whatever was here would probably get thrown out, anyway.

April went for the elevator, holding it open for the two security guards that were carrying a box each. Thankfully, she'd not been one to decorate or bring a bunch of personal stuff in to the office.

Laughter rose again as she thought about all the work she'd been doing. It would take another sucker like her or several more people to get it done. That and she didn't have a ton of notes on the biggest contract she was working on because she'd only just had a call with the client this morning.

They'd have a fun time sorting out her sticky notes on her desk that she'd used because sometimes even she had trouble figuring out what she wrote. That whole discovery call would have to be redone for them and most of her clients. They were going to be pissed.

Kayla and Evan would probably pull their business if not others, too. Loyalty from her friends would be great here because it would hit them where it hurt the most. She'd do the little bit of work she needed for Kayla for free anyway.

"Where are you parked?" one of the security guards asked.

"I have a car coming." She walked out of the elevator to the front door, confident that if the car wasn't there yet, then it was close.

Much to her joy, it was. The driver opened the trunk for her two boxes. April decided that today was the day she'd wait for the driver to open the door for her. It showed that she was more important than these two men thought she was. Not that their opinion mattered, but it still made her feel better.

Later, she'd come down from this anger and the world would once again let her know that she wasn't in control. Right now, she was going to enjoy it.

"To home, Mrs. Hawkins?" the driver asked.

"Yes, please." April settled back into her seat and thought about what she was going to say to Cade when he got home.

She wanted to text him, but he'd already left so many times because of the stuff with her. This wasn't going to change between now and when he got home from work, so she'd tell him then. The first thing she was going to do was change into comfortable clothes. Then she'd grab a pint of ice cream and find a good movie. This day and that job didn't deserve anymore of her thoughts on it.

"Mrs. Hawkins, please stay in the car for a moment while I handle this."

Confused, April unbuckled and slid to the middle seat so she could look out the window. The driver was standing in front of the car having a conversation with an older man. It took her a second, but when the man turned to look in the car, she knew who it was.

Mr. Hawkins himself had come out of hiding. Seizing the opportunity to get what information she could, April got out and walked to the men.

"What seems to be the problem here?" she asked.

"Mrs. Hawkins, I really suggest you return to the car. I cannot get in touch with your husband and he wouldn't want you out here right now."

"It's quite all right," she assured him. "I'm sure my father-in-law means me no harm, isn't that right?" She turned her best smile on him.

"Of course not. I just wanted to talk to my son, but I see that he isn't here. Perhaps you and I could talk instead?" He smiled at her, that wicked up to something smile that sent chills up your spine.

"I don't see why not," she forced out. It was about now that her fear kicked in, but the common sense that told her to run was a little late on showing up. "Come inside and I will make us some tea."

Mr. Hawkins followed her inside. The driver wasn't far behind them with her boxes. He looked torn about leaving her there with him.

"Please return to get my husband. I know he'll be happy his father came to see him," she told him. Hopefully, the man understood that she meant to go get Cade and not to wait for him.

He glanced between them quickly and then backed away. "I'll see if he's called back yet."

"Great, thank you." April watched him leave before turning to her father-in-law.

"I hope you don't think that playing the stupid little hostess is going to work for you." Mr. Hawkins had positioned himself between her and the door. "Once he leaves, you and I are going to go for a drive of our own."

She'd screwed up. That much was obvious to her now. She'd become one of those characters in a show that was too stupid to live.

Pulling out her phone, she sent a text to Cade before Mr. Hawkins snatched it from her, tossing it across the room.

"None of that is needed. My son will figure things out soon enough and see that you aren't right for him. You won't have to worry about it after today."

Genuine fear, like she'd never known, had her in a chokehold. Turns out her fight or flight response was neither. It was to freeze, rooted in the same spot with the danger.

"The driver is gone. Let's go." Mr. Hawkins reached out and grabbed her arm, pulling her out the door.

Lots of things went through her head, but she wasn't able to act on any of them. She could only press one hand to her stomach in the backseat of the car and apologized to her baby. Staying quiet, she watched for where they were headed and hoped that her message to Cade went through, telling him she loved him.

Chapter Twenty-Six
Cade

Cade sat at his mother's favorite restaurant and waited for her to show up. He hated being in here. It smelled of too much flowery perfume, the kind that older ladies wore, and his signal was terrible.

After almost an hour of waiting, Cade rose, dropped bills on the table to cover at least his drinks and make up for taking the table up for so long. The closer he got to the door to the restaurant, the more insistent the chimes were that were coming from his phone.

He waited until he was outside to open it. Several messages and missed calls from his driver, a few messages from his friends, and one from April. Smiling, he opened hers first.

> April: I love you. I'm so sorry.

Instead of making him feel better, he knew that something was wrong.

He called April but got no answer, setting off more alarm bells. Twice more he tried all ringing several times before going to voicemail.

He called his driver back before checking anything else. He was at April's beck and call today. Cade had driven himself.

"What's going on?" Cade demanded as soon as the man answered.

"I tried telling her not to, sir."

"Not to what?"

"Mr. Hawkins, your father, was at the house when I pulled up. Mrs. Hawkins wouldn't stay in the car and invited him in for tea. Then she told me to go find you. I'm almost to your office."

"Go back to the house now and don't leave her there alone. I'm on my way."

Cade ran to his car, not caring who might see him. As soon as he got in, he shouted for his phone to call Jake.

"Hey, man. What's up?" Jake answered the call.

"My father went to my house and April invited him in for fucking tea!" Cade was reeling. "What the fuck is wrong with her? My driver left, and no one was there with them. I'm on my way there now."

"Call me right back and let me know what's going on. I'll call everyone else."

He ended the call just in time for Catherine to call him.

"How was lunch with Mother?"

"She didn't show up. Father did though, at my house while I was here waiting for Mother! He's there alone with April now, Cat."

"I'm on my way."

"No." The call ended. "Shit," Cade swore.

Now he needed to worry about both of them. Cade swore at the traffic as he raced to get back to his house. His driver hadn't called him back yet, and he prayed that meant that he was there with them.

A block from his house, he hit more traffic and gave up on the car. Pulling over, he left it there and took off running. That was a problem for another time.

Running home, he was at the door in probably record time, throwing it open. "April!" he shouted.

No answer came. He tried calling her again but only reached voicemail. The door opened behind him and Cade spun, prepared to lose his mind on his father.

"Where is she?" Catherine asked.

"I don't fucking know," Cade shouted at her. He was losing his grip on all the emotions he'd shoved down deep, being overcome with fear for her.

"Have you called her?" Catherine asked.

Cade shot her a look that told her that was a dumb question.

"Fine," Catherine said. She walked in and began to look around. "I don't see that tea was ever started and her purse is here, Cade. I think we need to call the police."

He considered his options. As much as he didn't want to make what was happening public, he cared more about April's safety. "You're right."

His phone rang, and Cade pulled it out of his pocket, seeing Jake on the screen.

"She's not here."

"Shit. Sit tight. We are all on our way over."

He ended the call and turned to Catherine, who was across the room looking at something on the floor. "Everyone is on their way over," he told her.

"Cade..." she sounded scared.

"What is it?" He walked over to her, looking at where she was.

April's broken cell phone was on the floor. The screen shattered. He reached to touch it, and Catherine slapped his hand.

"What the fuck?" he asked.

"Evidence," Catherine told him. "It's evidence. Probably no one should come over here now."

Ryker arrived about that time and went immediately to Catherine, pulling her against him. "Is that hers?" he asked, pointing at the phone.

Cade nodded.

"Let's go outside. We need to preserve things in here, Cade."

Catherine stepped away from Ryker and waited for them to leave before her.

They stood out front and waited for everyone else to arrive.

"I'm going home. Bring everyone to the office to reconvene. I'll meet you there, going home first to see if Mother tried to stop by."

"I'll have everyone go straight there," Ryker said, pulling out his phone.

The driver finally arrived. "There's a terrible accident out there. I'm sorry it took me so long to get back from the office."

"Did you see them leave?" Cade demanded.

The man shook his head. "They were inside together when I left."

"Fuck!" Cade shouted at the sky.

"Come on, let's go." Ryker pushed him towards the car. "Can you take us back to the office?" he asked the driver.

He ran around to the driver's seat and climbed in, ready to go. It took a bit of effort on Ryker's part to get Cade into the car. He didn't want to leave in case she came back. Hell, he hadn't even searched the whole house yet.

"Get in. We will figure it out," Ryker pressed.

He finally gave in and climbed into the car. Everyone was meeting him, and they would help. The police would take too long sorting through shit to be of much help right now. He needed to find his father.

"Call your guy and tell him that Father is in town. He should be easier to track now that we know he's close, at least."

Ryker nodded and made his call. Cade half listened as he tried to think of what else he could do. He needed her to be okay, and that meant finding her. If she'd been hurt at all, Cade was going to lose his shit on his father. Hell, he was going to do it, anyway.

He ended the call. "He's on it. Said he'd call back if he found out anything."

Cade nodded. What else could he do?

Traffic was worse now than when he'd headed this way. They

were at a standstill and nowhere near the office. Cade tried calling his mother several times as they rode with the calls going directly to voicemail.

"Still off?" Ryker asked.

"She had to be helping him with this. She made it so they'd know where I was, and then he came and took her. What the fuck is wrong with both of them?"

The car was still not moving and Cade felt like he was missing something important by sitting here.

"Has Catherine called you yet?" Ryker asked.

"Not yet. But if she's in this traffic, then she probably isn't home yet."

"Try her," he suggested. "Something's off here."

That was exactly what he'd been thinking, too. Cade tried her number and while it wasn't off like his mother's, it rang and went to voicemail.

"Nothing," Cade confirmed to Ryker.

"I don't like this," Ryker agreed. "No one has seen her at the office either.

The car was moving again, finally. It felt better to be in motion, like they were doing something even though they weren't, really.

"Security footage," Ryker said. "She left with your father. Looks scared, but she left willingly with him."

Ryker held out his phone for Cade to watch the footage. "He wasn't forcing her," Cade breathed. That was a good thing.

Ryker pulled his phone back. "I'm going to have him check on Catherine's building. I don't like that we aren't hearing from her."

Cade knew the feeling of not being able to get in touch with the woman he loved, so he didn't push the issue of invading her privacy. This was about safety, and he should have thought to do the same.

Ryker typed quickly into his phone while cursing the traffic. After only a minute, he set it back down. "We'll know in a minute."

Cade felt like a vise was pushing all the air out of his lungs and keeping him from being able to catch his breath. He was so worried for April and the baby that he hadn't thought to check on his sister right away, and that made him feel like an even bigger piece of shit than he had earlier.

"Hello." Ryker answered the phone. "Are you sure?"

"Change in plans. We're going to Catherine's right now," Ryker said.

Chapter Twenty-Seven
April

April had gone quietly along with Mr. Hawkins and so far, other than listening to his ranting and raving, she was okay. He had been on a kick the entire car ride about how she had corrupted his son and that everyone else was doing the same.

They had shown up at Catherine's apartment, and she'd been floored. Immediately, she wondered if Catherine was involved in everything until she showed up.

Currently, Catherine was trying to convince her mother that something was wrong with this situation, but she was completely devoted to her husband and there would be no convincing her otherwise. It was a lost cause, April could see it, but Catherine pressed anyway.

"Shut up!" Mr. Hawkins finally yelled.

"You've also been a poor daughter, corrupted by these so-called friends of yours. They are making you think you are more than what you are. A daughter's job is to marry well and until then, she is supposed to take care of her parents."

Catherine snorted. "A daughter would need to have been shown how to take care of people in order to do that to others. I guess you two forgot about the raising your own children part?"

If her goal was to make her father have a heart attack, she was well on her way to it. Mr. Hawkins looked like he was going to explode and was getting redder by the second.

"Sit down next to her now. We will see both of my problems taken care of today. Don't think anyone hasn't noticed the way you chase after that Ryker guy."

Catherine looked confused, but joined April on her sofa. "Cade will be here soon," she whispered.

"No whispering," her mother fussed.

"As I was saying before, I was interrupted. I am trying to do right by my wife and make sure the children that we have together been the best children they can be, but you're making it difficult. First thing we need is for you to leave." His eyes focused on April. "You can go wherever you want, but you must never return. I will leave you a nice sum of money to do it."

"He's my husband," April countered. "And we're having a baby." She regretted reminding him of the baby as soon as she did.

"That's the other thing. Take the brat with you. It never returns here either, and neither of you are to contact my son. You have nothing for you here anymore, so you might as well take the money and go because the settlement you will get in a divorce won't be as nice." He smiled like he had everything figured out.

"Cade wouldn't let her just disappear. Do you not even know your own son? He loves her and the baby. Nothing would stop him from finding her. April is better than that anyway and wouldn't take your money." Catherine stood up again, yelling this time.

"Sit down, girl. We will get on the matter of you in a moment." He ignored Catherine. "Now, are you going to go willingly, or do I need to have someone escort you? Everyone has a price and I promise what I am offering you is the best deal you're going to get."

"I'm not leaving Cade." April folded her arms, feeling every bit the defiant child, and this wasn't even her father.

"The hard way it is. I'll have you know the fee for having someone escort you comes out of the money I would have given you and he isn't cheap."

"You really should just go along. It will be safer and easier," Mrs. Hawkins said.

"Cade and I will not go along with this stupid plan of yours. What the hell is wrong with you?" Catherine shouted at her father. "If you think either of us would want to, then you're crazier than we gave you credit for."

"Your brother will see things my way. You'll see. If he doesn't, then it's the last hope for your mother to have obedient children. I have other children who are ready and waiting to do what needs done without so much fighting."

Catherine paled and sat back on the couch. April reached over and took her hand, both of them squeezing tight.

"See, here's where you're wrong. Anyone given massive amounts of money will eventually turn on you and get tired of doing your bidding," came Cade's menacing voice from the doorway.

Ryker was right behind him and looked murderous. "I sure would be curious who these other children are, though. I think I have a lead."

"Ha! You're just a fool who got lucky once and made some money. You are of no concern to me and need to stay away from my daughter," Mr. Hawkins had stopped yelling and turned completely calm at the arrival of the men.

"You need to step away from them, Father," Cade said, making slow steps in her direction.

"You need to be a better son. I have given you everything and I will not have you behave as though you have no sense," Mrs. Hawkins was saying.

"Shut up, Mother. Stop going on with what he says. Can't you see that he's losing his mind?" Catherine cried out for her mother.

"Catherine, let it go," Cade said evenly.

April looked back to him to see he and Ryker had separated, both giving his parents a wide berth, but they were slowly approaching.

"If you don't listen and do as I say, I will end her and the baby that you don't need. You can support them both from afar, but there is no need for you to be married to her! She wasn't the right one, and you messed everything up." His wild moods were scaring her, the way he went from calm to shouting and threatening her and the baby told her he would do it.

"Is that what you did?" Cade asked.

"Of course it is. That whore was supposed to be on birth control, but no, she just had to give me a set of twins. Didn't tell me until after they were born. I set them all up real nice and I have two other obedient children that I can start over with."

"And how would you do that?" Cade asked. "I kind of run a company and I feel like people would miss me."

"You wouldn't disappear, you'd be dead. If you can't fix this, then I will be, so it's me or you."

"Fix what. What did you do?" Cade pressed.

"All you had to do was marry the right fucking bitch. That's it! Now I have to have someone else do it and you have no heir to pass the company on to, so I guess my next in line will have to do," he smiled smugly.

"You know that's not how this works, right? The company isn't family owned. They would be free to find a new CEO," Cade pointed out.

"You're wrong," his father's voice turned menacing. "I could just kill you now and solve all of my problems. The baby too. No one would miss him." He pointed at Ryker. "And Catherine would come around, eventually."

"That's enough, Mr. Hawkins," came another voice from the doorway.

Several police filed in as Cade and Ryker ran to the women. Cade lifted her off the sofa and hugged her tightly, before pulling back to look her over.

"Are you hurt?" he asked.

April shook her head. "He just threatened and talked."

"If you ever do something so foolish again, I don't know what I'll do." He pulled her into his chest again, holding her tight.

To their left, a weird reunion was happening between Catherine and Ryker. She turned back to face Cade's chest, giving them a bit of privacy, but had plans to ask Catherine about that later.

"Do you know who I am?" Mr. Hawkins was shouting.

It was almost comical in that cliche way of rich men thinking they were above the law. His wife was being cuffed as well, though she was being surprisingly quiet.

"We know exactly who you are and that's why we're here. Ms. Hawkins has security cameras everywhere, so soon a judge and jury will know who you are, too."

"Best thing I ever did," Catherine added.

Cade reached over and pulled her away from Ryker, holding her tight with one arm and April with the other.

"I'm so glad you're both safe," he whispered.

"You will need to stay somewhere else for a while, Ms. Hawkins. We have to tape this off as a crime scene and we will need everyone's statements."

It took hours to get through all the questions. They each gave their statement to several officers before they were able to leave. Catherine was coming home with them and it seemed that Ryker was going to as well. April didn't question it, happy that everyone was safe now.

Both of their parents were arrested there and taken off. Catherine was already fielding reporters and had given a statement that there would be no statement from the family at this time. Ryker nearly took a few out as they left the apartment building and swarms of reporters came after Catherine. She managed them with perfection, as she was so good at.

They returned to Cade's house and had dinner with everyone over before settling in for the night. Catherine was still downstairs, working, but she and Cade had headed upstairs for bed. Work was her distraction, even though it had to do with what she was distracting herself from. Cade had tried to talk her into going to bed, but she wouldn't have any of it.

They laid in bed next to each other, Cade's arm around her, just existing. April was the first one to break the silence.

"Do you think he really had another family somewhere?" she asked.

"I do. I'll work with Ryker and we'll find them and see if they can be helped. I'm sure there's a trail of his support that we can find."

"I just can't imagine treating your children the way your parents did tonight or having a whole second family." April rubbed her stomach as she thought of the little one in there.

Cade sighed and turned on his side to face her. "I'd never do that to you," he told her.

"I know." She leaned over and pressed a soft kiss to his lips. What she had learned during today's events was that she did trust Cade and believe him when he said he wanted this to be forever.

"Did you mean what you said today?" Cade asked.

April tried to figure out what he meant. So much had happened in less than a day, really. "What?"

"So forgettable then?" He laughed before turning serious. "The text you sent. You told me you loved me. Did you mean it?"

She relaxed. "Of course I meant it. I love you, Cade. I want this to be real and forever." She held her breath as she waited for him to say something.

"Thank God. I love you, too, April. This has always been real for me, before I even knew it was."

His mouth covered hers and April melted into him. He deepened the kiss, and she thought she'd never get enough of this man, her husband.

Chapter Twenty-Eight
Cade

Cade and Catherine sat in the front of the courtroom behind the prosecution as they waited for the verdict on his parents. It had been a quick trial even though it had taken months to get started, but he was confident that they'd done enough to convict them.

What his parents really needed was support. Someone to tell them that everything they were thinking didn't make sense. They had chosen not to accept a plea deal for it and instead it had gone to trial.

Both of them had tried to get information from their parents about their missing siblings, but neither had come forward. Cade had also pressed to see if there was anything he could find out about the plans that Cade had supposedly ruined, not wanting to be blindsided by something else, but again, they'd both remained quiet.

He was surprised, but he was annoyed. To think that these were his parents, and they were prepared to get rid of their grandchild and daughter-in-law. At the end, they both seemed pretty willing to end Cade's life as well.

It was hard to imagine thinking of your children like that. Cade's child wasn't here yet, and he was already certain he would do anything for him. April had her scan yesterday, and they'd gotten to see a glimpse of their little one, a boy, that would be joining them soon.

April didn't come to any of the trial which hadn't needed any witnesses. The cameras that were in Catherine's old apartment had been damning enough without anything else. Then the cops had overheard the threats, and that was really it.

Catherine squeezed his hand as the verdict was ready.

"We, the jury, find the defendants guilty."

Cade struggled to breathe. There were multiple charges, and he listened as each one came back with a guilty verdict. It was finally over for them. A sad ending, but an ending nonetheless.

"You did this and now it's all your problem. Good luck dealing with him," his father shouted at Cade before laughing hysterically.

Cade rose and took Catherine's arm, escorting her from the courtroom. There was no need to stick around for anything else. Sentencing would happen another day, and he didn't need to hear any more of his father's outbursts.

"What do you think he's talking about?" Catherine asked.

"I don't know. The real question is if it's even real. Everything he's said could just be a figment of his imagination and whatever he has going on in there." Cade shrugged. They'd just have to wait and see.

"We're going to find them, though?" she asked, referring to their siblings.

"We are going to do all we can," he promised.

Cade's car was waiting for them outside the back of the courthouse, where they were able to avoid most of the reporters. Catherine kept her calm with the ones that showed up while Cade took deep breaths until he was in the car.

"It's all fine, you know? They are just doing their job."

"Maybe, but I don't like it. They should get different jobs," Cade grumped.

"I think you need your wife. You're getting grouchy, which means you've been away from her for too long," Catherine teased.

She thought it was a joke, but she was right. He wanted April near him, keeping him calm and level-headed while this mess continued.

"Hopefully, this will be old news in the next week or so. I'm tired of dealing with it and it's messing up my own work." Catherine sighed as she relaxed into the seat.

Catherine hadn't been able to go on camera for any of her clients since the arrests. The reporters would always spin things back on her and her parents, and she couldn't effectively do her job. She'd taken a step back from it but Cade knew she hated that.

"Want me to drop you off first?" Cade offered.

She shook her head. "I'm borrowing your driver for the rest of the day to look at homes." She had been staying with them, refusing to go back to her apartment, and was ready to move out again.

"You know you can stay as long as you want. Neither of us mind," he told her.

"I know. You two have been great, but it's time. I'll find something soon. I hope." Catherine scrolled through her phone.

He knew her enough to know that when she put her mind to something, there was no changing it, so he let it go. Hopefully, she stayed picky and found something she really liked.

April was waiting for him when he opened his front door. Her arms reaching around both him and the baby belly she'd grown to hug him.

"I'm so sorry," she said.

"It needed to happen." He rested his chin on her head as he held his growing family close. "I love you."

"I love you too, Cade."

He stepped back and knelt before her, his face eye level with her baby bump. "I love you, too, little one." He was rewarded with a big kick.

April laughed. "I think he loves you, too, daddy."

Keep in touch with Toni Denise

Follow Toni Denise on Social Media!
Facebook
Instagram
Twitter
And Sign up for her Newsletter to find out about awesome games
and new releases.
Sign up here!

Owen

Don't miss the prequel novella, Owen's story.

Owen is a man who always knows and gets what he wants, but when he goes to the bar to grab a nightcap, he gets more than he bargained for. He meets a woman who's unlike any he's ever known but saying goodbye to bachelorhood will take some convincing.

Jenna isn't thrilled with the idea of going on a blind date, but a deal is a deal, so she shows up. She meets a great guy, who saves her from what would've been a disastrous date. Unfortunately, she never hears from him again.

Even though, the unplanned date goes well, Owen has a big decision to make. Is Jenna the one who will make him rethink bachelorhood?

Find out what happens in the prequel novella to the Billionaire Blind Date Series!

To read the full story, sign up for my newsletter!
www.tonidenisebooks.com

Owen Chapter 1

Owen stepped into The Striped Keg bar and looked around. The dim lighting was a stark contrast to the well-lit street he had just come in from.

Men and women chatted throughout the room, most standing at tables with a few lining the bar. He came here specifically to avoid too much conversation. Plus, as it was across town, no one recognized him.

They could if they looked hard enough, but few ever did, and that was what he wanted. A drink and some peace.

Walking around the old wooden bar, he took a seat at the far end and waited for the bartender to notice him. It had been a disastrous week, one he'd like to forget, and here where he blended in, it helped.

"What can I get ya?" the bartender asked.

He handed over his card. "Start a tab. I have a ride home, didn't drive here. Scotch."

He always made it a point to let the bartender know he wasn't driving. It helped make sure he wasn't cut off before he was done for the night.

"All right." With a curt nod the bartender walked away.

"Excuse me?" A pretty blonde in a black dress approached him. "Are you Kyle?"

Owen shook his head.

"Damn. Mind if I sit here?" she asked as she set her small purse on the bar and sat down without waiting for an answer. "Why I let my sister set me up on some stupid blind date with a guy name Kyle of all things, I'll never know. Then he's not even here on time? Way to set the tone."

As much as he didn't want to be, he had to admit he was intrigued by the plain-speaking woman next to him. She didn't even seem to care if anyone was listening to her monologue, just kept on going.

The bartender brought Owen's drink over and turned to the woman.

"A beer, please. Whatever's on tap is fine."

"Add it to my tab," Owen said without thinking.

It was stupid. She was going to sit here now and keep talking to him and there went all hope for his night of peace.

"You don't have to do that," she told him as the bartender walked away.

"Looks like you could use a good break tonight, figured maybe it would cheer you up."

"I'm not going to sleep with you," she said boldly, causing Owen to choke on his first sip.

"What?"

"Just because you bought me a drink and my date didn't show, I'm not so grateful that I'll drop my panties for you tonight. I don't do one-night stands."

Owen couldn't hold back the bark of laughter that spilled out. "You're very blunt," he told her.

"No sense in not saying what you mean here in a dark bar with strangers. If you want, I can pay for my drink myself when he comes back with it."

"It's okay. I don't mind paying for it with nothing in return." He flashed his most charming smile at her. "I didn't intend to get anything for it as it was."

"Thank you."

Her drink showed up a moment later and he let the bartender know she was on his tab until he closed out.

"Why'd you think I was your date?"

"Wishful thinking, perhaps?" She shook her head at herself before turning back to him. "You were late getting here and your tie is the right color."

"My tie?" It was a light green, one he wore often, favoring the color.

"Yeah, he's supposed to be wearing a green tie. That's vague enough, but what shade of green? There's so many, and then so many men in here with green ties."

He nodded as he listened to her ramble on about ties. She was animated when she talked, and he found himself enjoying it and her company. Normally he carried the conversations but didn't feel the need to with her.

"Sorry," she said suddenly.

"For what?" He tilted his head, trying to figure out what happened.

"I always talk too much. It's a fault of mine and annoys people." She sipped her beer as though that was making it all better because she couldn't talk.

"Oddly enough, I was enjoying your speech on ties and the various colors of green."

"Liar," she said but then grinned up at him.

"I am in a position where I don't want to be the only one talking but I seem to always be doing just that. Having someone I don't need to pretend I want to do all the talking with is refreshing."

"Well, flattery will get you everywhere," she laughed. "Except my bed."

"Got it. Not sleeping together tonight."

She shook her head but laughed.

"Excuse me, are you Jenna?" A man in a poor-fitting suit stood next to her.

Still facing him, he could see the indecision on her face as she looked back at who had to be Kyle. He looked like a jerk and was definitely older than both of them.

Finally, she answered, "I am. Are you Kyle?"

He nodded and then didn't even bother to hide it as he checked her out from head to toe. "Must be my lucky night. You are stunning."

Owen rolled his eyes and sipped his scotch. This guy was going to get nowhere with her and he was interested in watching it happen.

"Sorry, if you were looking for a hookup, let me save you the time. I won't be sleeping with you for at least a few months, if you last that long."

Thank God he had already swallowed his drink or he would have choked on it again. Owen let a small smile sneak out as he watched Kyle try to decide what to say to that.

"Months?" Kyle asked, the shock evident on his face.

"At least three, maybe six," Jenna confirmed.

"Umm, well, I," Kyle stammered and pulled at his collar.

Taking pity on him, Owen jumped into the conversation. "Dude, just cut your losses and find a new bar and date."

Kyle seemed to just register his presence as his gaze slid to Owen. "I mean, it's not that we had to tonight, but like, that's a long time."

Owen just shook his head. "Go on."

Kyle seemed slightly relieved as he spun and disappeared into the crowded bar.

"You really should have let him sweat it out a bit longer."

"Couldn't. The man looked like he was going to pop before he ever managed a sentence."

"A pity he was only looking to get laid. I'm never letting my sister set me up again. Where'd she even meet him?"

Owen laughed. "He looks like a used car salesman, and not a very good one."

Jenna threw her head back and laughed. "God, yes. That's exactly it."

"Months, huh?' Owen arched an eyebrow at her.

"For him? Absolutely. If ever." She looked at her phone. "He's almost an hour late and was clearly checking me out before he decided if he wanted to have the date. It's going to be a no, bud."

"Bud?" Owen teased.

"He looks like he calls people bud."

He agreed and nodded. The man one hundred percent looked like he did. "Well, now that you have no date tonight, what are you going to do?"

"You're not my date?" Jenna fake pouted before giggling. "Don't look so horrified. I'm not trying to trap you."

"Not horrified, more curious," he answered simply. "So what was supposed to happen on this date?" Curious now, he found he wanted to keep the conversation going and know more about her.

"I assumed we'd chat over drinks and decide if we wanted a second date. Didn't really think about it that deep to be honest."

"What a crummy date," Owen said.

"I agree. I really should have just stayed home."

"Now, that I wouldn't have agreed with."

Just then Kyle walked by again. "Months," he muttered, shaking his head before turning into the crowd again.

"Dude's a creep," Owen observed. "Want to get out of here?" he asked her.

Jenna pinned him with a look that had him backpedaling.

"To get pizza. I swear. It's walking distance, too."

She stared at him for a moment, and he knew she was deciding whether to believe him or not before she nodded.

"Bartender!" Owen called. "I think we're ready to pay." So much for the tab he'd been planning to run up.

Liked it? Get it for free by signing up for my newsletter at www. tonidenisebooks.com

Coming Next

Check out the next two books in the series
Ryker
Luke

Also by Toni Denise

Learn More or get buy links for any of these books at my author website:

tonidenisebooks.com

Westbeach Series:
Old Friends
On the Run
One Last Chance
Out of Time
Series Boxset

Finding Love Series:
Engaged to Her Neighbor
Married to the Playboy
Falling for Her Fake Husband

Short and Steamy Duet:
The Wedding Date

Bonus Content Old Friends

Sometimes a second chance can be the last chance.

Recently divorced, Kelly finds herself back in her hometown. Deciding that starting over is key, she and her son take to living a new life.

When a second chance with Mason, an old flame, ignites, Kelly is excited to feel love again.

But something is wrong. Someone is watching them, waiting to strike. Someone that knows them. Someone. . . close.

Not knowing who she can trust, Kelly is thrust into a life of fear and looking over her shoulder.

Where do you turn when the one person you thought you could trust might actually be the person you're running from?

A steamy romance novel with a moderate heat level, free on all platforms!

Old Friends Chapter 1

Taking in the scenery, Kelly wondered why she never came back to visit. Going home was hard, but it was only about a four-hour drive. She really should have come home before now. Taking the long road around the outside of town, the scenery alternated between trees so dense the automatic headlights came on in her car and open pastures with cows or horses in them. This time of year, everything was still bright green. It looked pretty, but she knew better; being late August, it was hot out there. Soon the brilliant green would give way to a wonder of colors as fall slowly crept in.

Turning the music down, she focused on the GPS and the last few miles of her trip. Traffic had started to pick up in the previous hour of her journey until she left the interstate. She was glad she had left earlier in the day; it was only about 4:00 p.m. now. A quick check of the back seat showed Hunter was waking up. For a seven-year-old, he wasn't a bad road-trip partner, but he had slept all but the first hour, when he ate most of the snacks. "Hey, Hunt, we're almost there. Are you excited?"

"Are we in a zoo?" Hunter sleepily asked.

Kelly took another look around, wondering why this was even a question. Cows. There were cows on both sides of the road. "No, baby, there are ranches around here that raise cows."

"So, I'll see the zoo every day?"

"Yes." Simpler to agree than to explain more as he wasn't awake yet. Besides, in all his seven years, he'd never seen the countryside, and Westbeach was about as opposite of DC as you could get.

As they made the last turn, the woods on either side were a welcome presence, adding shade to the last bit of the trip, which had been mostly on the sunny highway. She was going to have a sunglasses tan for sure. Finally pulling in to the driveway, Kelly breathed a sigh of relief to see her aunt and uncle already there and waiting for them.

The light blue house was one level and had a small new porch on the front. The wood was still white looking, so she could tell it hadn't been there long. The front yard was freshly cut, and there were trees on both sides of the property and behind it. A privacy fence, which also looked new, wrapped around the backyard. No neighbors could be seen unless you were in the road. *Wonder if I'll be able to sleep without the noise of the city?*

Aunt Mary was the first to come off the porch as Kelly parked the car. Mary, in her signature flower dress and floppy hat over her white hair, had always been able to style anything except herself. Her dresses were like something older ladies probably wore in the fifties. Gardening, cooking, shopping—same dresses; some things never changed. Bob, on the other hand, was a jeans and T-shirt man. Kelly could never remember Uncle Bob having hair—on his head or face. Much like Mary though, his style was the same no matter what he was doing. The only thing these two changed was the colors each day.

When Kelly stepped out of her car, Aunt Mary immediately wrapped her in a welcoming hug. "How are you doin', dear? How was the trip?"

"Let her get out of the car, Mary." Uncle Bob always sounded a tad sour but was a sweetheart underneath.

"I am, I am." Aunt Mary backed up and opened the back door for Hunter to climb out of the car. "Hunter! You've gotten so big!" Hunter grinned and stood tall at her praise. Mary ruffled his hair and proceeded to go to the trunk with Uncle Bob to get their bags. "Is this all you brought, honey?"

"For now. The rest is packed, and Dylan is supposed to send it this week, but we'll see if he remembers to let the movers in or not."

"Okay, let us know if you forgot anything." Aunt Mary smiled sadly at Kelly.

"You know I will." She plastered on a big smile to reassure everyone that she really was okay. Taking Hunter's hand, she turned and walked into the house.

When she walked in, the first thing she noticed was that the house was fully furnished; some things even looked new. A gray sofa in the living room faced a flat-screen TV with a small coffee table. Passing through the living room to the kitchen, she noticed there was a cherry-colored table for four with a bouquet of fresh flowers waiting for them. *Definitely Aunt Mary's idea.* And the smell—some version of every spice, but in a good way—was just like Bob and Mary's house. It was a welcoming scent, the smell of home.

Kelly walked down the hall of the modest one-story house, pulling her suitcase behind her. Three rooms, two bathrooms—per Mary's directions, hers was the last on the left. The room had a large queen-sized bed in the center with a gorgeous purple quilt and matching pillows on it. A dresser sat against the long wall with a mirror attached.

Checking all the doors, she discovered the closet was behind the open bedroom door, and against the wall was a master bath. A purple shower curtain hung already with silver bath mats. Aunt Mary really should have been an interior designer, and her remembering Kelly's favorite color just made it that much better.

Kelly had never been able to have everything decorated in her favorite color before, but now she could do her thing. Putting her bag down she took a deep breath; divorce wasn't going to be too bad if this was how it started. Coming back home wasn't all that bad, even if it did make her feel a little like a failure for her marriage not working.

There was no love lost in her marriage anyway. Dylan didn't even fight for custody of Hunter. He just let them go and agreed to everything—not that she had asked for much, just child support and custody. Dylan didn't even want weekends with Hunter. Kelly sighed as she looked in the mirror and pulled her hair into a ponytail before heading back out to the other three noisily chatting about cows in the dining room.

"Hunter tells me he's excited to see the zoo every day," Uncle Bob informed her with a laugh as he pulled Kelly up for a quick hug. Although pushing seventy, Bob was still a tall man. He was the exact opposite of Mary, who was shorter than Kelly by five inches, standing at five feet tall. The family had always joked that it was her hat that gave her an inch or two and that she genuinely was less than five feet. Mary had always laughed along as well, shushing everyone, but never argued it.

"Something tells me he'll eventually tire of it," Kelly said with a small laugh of her own.

"I stocked some essentials in the cabinets and fridge; wasn't sure what all you would need. We can go to dinner later, or you can come over and I'll cook." Aunt Mary always made sure everyone had eaten. If you weren't hungry, she was going to have you doing something until you were. "We are waiting on the handyman though. The disposal isn't working right now."

"No problem, and we can eat whatever is easiest for you tonight. Thank you guys again." Bending down, she hugged Aunt Mary again and gave her a kiss on the cheek. "I don't know what I would do without you guys here."

"Family helps family, dear." And that was all Aunt Mary was going to say about it. No thanks needed ever.

"I love you." Before either of them did more than tear up, Kelly changed the subject. "The handyman? Is that who redid the front porch? It looks nice."

"Yes, yes. Bob thought he was going to do it. Took the boards off and then decided it was too much for one old man, like I said." She cut a look at Bob, who decided not to say anything and continued to talk to Hunter. "Thankfully," Mary continued, "the handyman was able to get out here and get it done before you got here."

"Really?" Hunter shouted and jumped up from the table to run out the back door.

"I told him there was a swing set out there." Bob smiled and moved to follow Hunter out the door.

"He will never come inside again." Kelly laughed and moved to the window to see Hunter happily swinging while Uncle Bob looked on.

"Go unpack, and I'll wait right here for the doorbell," Mary said while shooing Kelly from the window. "He'll be fine."

"I know. I'll be in his room for now if you need me."

Wandering down the hall, Kelly opened the door across from her room and was pleased to find an office. Mary really had thought of everything. A small desk sat facing the window with a fancy-looking high-backed office chair, and she could see the entire backyard from there. A tall lamp in the corner would keep her from having to turn on the overhead light to see, and a ceiling fan was a nice addition. The room was painted a darker shade of blue, but it didn't seem to make the room feel smaller.

There was plenty of room left in there for her treadmill since there was no gym here that she knew of, and going for a run would be difficult with Hunter still home for the summer. Mary always knew what worked and what didn't without even trying. Kelly would be glad to get back to work in two weeks in her new office. Thankfully, her legal transcription was work from home, and they had been generous with her time off under the circumstances. She would have a pile of work when she got back to it though. It was going to be rough going back to work after all this time off. Thinking about her emails that she hadn't checked all day, she walked out of the room and closed the door.

Moving on, Kelly checked the room next to hers and saw a twin bed, some toys already set out for Hunter, and a large baseball poster on the wall across from her. Smiling, she walked over and touched it, amazed by the little things Bob and Mary had thought of to help Hunter adjust. She'd also bet money that there was no swing set here before Kelly decided to move in. Kelly heaved Hunter's suitcase on the bed and started to unpack and put away the clothes.

"I didn't pack hangers." Kelly let out a deep sigh. "If this is the worst part, I'm good, right?" Musing to herself, she walked down the hall to see if Mary wanted to go to the store. "Mary, are you interested in running to the—" Seeing a man in the kitchen, Kelly stopped midsentence.

"Kelly, this is Mason, the handyman. Mason, do you remember Kelly?"

"How could I forget?" Drying his hands off, he looked up, and Kelly stared into eyes she hadn't seen in twelve years. Mason Cole.

"Wow! How are you? It's been forever." Not sure what to do with herself, she leaned awkwardly against the wall, taking in this man who had been a teenager when she saw him last. Instead, here was this man with his dark brown hair and muscles she could see through his blue shirt. And those blue eyes... a woman could get lost in those eyes. He hadn't changed much other than getting older, like her she supposed. He was still as handsome as ever.

"How's the set working out?" Mason interrupted Kelly's assessment of him. Oh, that smile, crooked with one dimple on the right cheek. That smile could make women fall all over themselves to get a glimpse of it. Nope, that hadn't changed one bit.

"Hunter is already out there." Mary saved her from having to form an answer. Nothing could have prepared Kelly for seeing this man in her kitchen.

Swallowing down old feelings and trying to move forward, Kelly shifted to look out the window on the back door to see Hunter still outside playing. Taking it in for the first time, she noticed the back deck was only slightly above ground level, just one step up. *I need to get a table and chairs for out here, so I can work and watch Hunter play.* The yard was a fair size, plenty of room for Hunter to run around, and the start of the tree line had been fenced into the yard, giving him a shaded place to play. The swing set was a good size as well, containing two swings, a slide, and monkey bars on one end. Uncle Bob strolled from the deck to the yard, watching Hunter wear himself out. *At least he'll sleep tonight, even after that long nap in the car.*

"What did you need, dear?" Aunt Mary asked.

"Oh, I didn't pack hangers and was wondering where the closest store was?" She focused on Mary, anything to not stare at this too-hot-to-be-here man in the kitchen.

"That would still be Gersham's down on Main Street. I have to head there to order the part for your disposal if you'd like a ride?" Of course, it was Mason who answered. And a ride, really? Lord knew she wanted to go for a ride. Wait, where had that thought come from? How unlike her; must be the nerves.

"I don't want to impose. I can head down there later."

"No imposing at all. Grab your bag and hop in the truck." Interesting how the words he chose said he made the decision, but the tone made it clear it was still her call.

Grabbing her bag, she let Hunter know she would be right back. For all he cared though, he was still enthralled with the swings and slide out back. After hugging Aunt Mary, she walked out to the dark blue Dodge Ram sitting in her driveway. Mason was standing by the truck and opened the door for her. He waited until she had settled before closing it. *What am I supposed to say now? What do I do?* Placing her bag in her lap, she sat still as he climbed in and backed out the driveway. Not much was said on the way to the store.

Staring out the passenger window, she watched the scenery. Everything seemed the same, and yet it all seemed so different at the same time. When they got to the store, they went their separate ways after Mason pointed her in the right direction. She grabbed several packs of hangers and headed toward the checkout. Mason was already standing there putting in an order for whatever part it was he needed.

As she approached, a shiver ran down her spine. Kelly felt like someone was watching her. Looking around, she didn't see anyone else in the store besides Mason and the clerk. Still, she picked up her pace, unable to shake the creepy feeling. She set the hangers on the counter, continuing to look around while waiting for them to finish. *You're losing it. No one is in here, just the empty store getting you creeped out.*

Needing a distraction, she watched the interaction going on at the register. The woman was practically hanging on Mason's every word like she was super interested in garbage disposals. Kelly rolled her eyes. When she looked up again, Mason winked at her. She had been caught. Completely distracted from the creepy feeling, she now had a new one—full-on embarrassment.

Part ordered and hangers paid for, they walked back to the truck again. Mason took the awkward bags of hangers and opened her door for her. While Kelly buckled in, he put the bags in the back seat, then shut her door and got in.

"Didn't like her much, did you?"

Kelly felt the heat creep up her face. He wasn't going to ignore her eye roll. "It wasn't that. More of a disbelief type of thing." *There, that makes me sound less rude for not liking someone I don't even know and positively not jealous.*

"Nope, it's been a while, but you still can't hide anything. It's all over your face," he teased.

Kelly put her hand to her heart and leaned toward Mason, doing an exaggerated impersonation of the busty clerk. "Oh, please tell me more about garbage disposals." She batted her lashes. "I just don't know what I would do without you having come in today, Mason." Kelly laughed and sat back right in the seat.

"Pretty good impression actually. Now you know why I didn't want to go to the store alone." Mason cut her a sly look but laughed as well. After a moment, they both fell into a companionable silence for the rest of the trip. Pulling up, Mason stopped her from opening the door with a hand on her shoulder. "It's good to see you and have you home again, even if it's not under the best of circumstances."

"Thank you. I'm glad to be home. No love lost in the reason for my coming home, so no worries. I'm glad I got to see you."

"If you need anything while you're here, let me give you my number. Your aunt and uncle call when something needs to be done in one of their rentals. Most of your new home has been newly renovated though; they really went all out to make it right for you. Oh, and I'll let Bob know when the part comes in. She said Tuesday, but when I pick it up will depend on when I can get someone to go to the store with me." Mason laughed again.

"I noticed. The porch looks great, and the swing set too. If you let me know when the part is ready, I can run in and pick it up, and then you can avoid the store altogether." Kelly winked at him. "You can just let me know. Let me find a paper, and I'll give you my number." She dug through her bag and came up with a crayon and a receipt. Blushing again at how much of a mess she must seem, she wrote her number down and handed it to him. Saying their goodbyes, she hopped out of the truck and went inside with a smile on her face.

\#

Kelly Marie Holstead, he didn't know she would be there today. He could have sworn it was tomorrow that Mary said she would get here. Pulling into his own driveway, he smiled as he remembered Kelly's reaction to Darlene, the clerk at Gersham's. Just like the old Kelly would have done, she let loose with that cute little eye roll. Heading inside, he greeted Shep, his aging yellow lab, with a pat on the head. Shep followed him through the house, waiting to be let outside. Grabbing a beer from the fridge, Mason opened the back door and went out to the deck, Shep in tow.

Checking his phone, he texted Nate, his brother and business partner, about the disposal and the part needed. He pulled Kelly's crayon-written number out of his pocket and plugged it into his phone. *Should I text her now, so she has my number? Is it too soon?*

After deciding to just program the number in and debate it later, his thoughts wandered to the day he had. After a rough morning with two young guys late to work, again, he was frustrated and cranky when he remembered he was supposed to check on Kelly's disposal today. When he pulled up, he was in no mood for small talk with Mary but had resigned himself to it. Then he noticed another car in the driveway.

Kelly apparently hadn't been expecting him. He wasn't entirely expecting her either. He hadn't seen her in almost twelve years, since they were seventeen and about to graduate high school. That summer was some of the best memories he had though. Kelly was his best friend, but when they went to college in different states, they had slowly lost touch. It was one of his biggest regrets. He and Kelly had shared everything—sometimes too much, but he could always tell her anything, and she, him. He knew Kelly had gotten married right after she graduated college, and that was about it.

She still looked as good as ever, a more mature woman and no longer the body of a teenager, but time had been kind to her. Her blonde hair had been pulled back, but it was more than shoulder length and had some highlights. Her body though, she looked like she took care of herself; he could see her defined leg muscles under her shorts. Her curves were more significant than he remembered. She wore no makeup, probably not something she usually did, but no reason to get dolled up for a road trip to move. He liked the no makeup look though, no pretending, nothing to hide.

Just then his phone went off, pulling him out of his thoughts as they headed in the wrong direction. Texting Nate back, he got up, adjusted his pants, and Shep followed him in the door. Nate was going to give him a hard time about seeing Kelly, and about venturing into Gersham's when he knew Darlene would be working. He wasn't kidding; he had taken Kelly as a bit of a buffer. Darlene always shamelessly threw herself at him, but she'd limit it to flirting if there was someone else in the store. The woman never took the hint that he wasn't interested, even though he had tried to let her down gently many times before. Now he just avoided the place when he knew she was working.

Time to make dinner. Pulling out the chicken, he got started on cooking. *Wonder if she still cooks as well as she used to?* What the hell was he doing, thinking about her so much? It had only been a few minutes, and nothing had even happened to make him feel so much about her. She hadn't thrown herself at him like most women, so what was it?

Finishing up dinner, he carried it to the living room. Watching TV would distract his wayward thoughts.

\#

He waited in his car with the lights off until Mason had finally left Kelly's house. He had watched her from the back of the store as she searched hangers. He couldn't believe she had been home just a few hours and was already back with Mason. How had that happened? Had to be her meddling aunt. He had been watching the house for the past week waiting for her arrival and would meet her again soon. She was supposed to come back after she finished school, and like a fool, he had expected her to, but no, she went and got married and hadn't come back at all.

He had followed her online for a long time and had made sure she found out about her husband's cheating. Chuckling to himself, he remembered how easy that had been. He had just pretended to be the secretary's doctor and called their house phone looking for the father of the baby. Of course, Kelly had answered. Then he "accidentally" spilled the news of the baby to her. He had gotten her home now. She hadn't been happy in her marriage anyway, so he didn't feel bad. This time, she would be his, and neither Mason nor anything else was going to stand in his way. He carefully put away his phone, excited to have new photos of her on it, and headed home.

www.ingramcontent.com/pod-product-compliance
Lightning Source LLC
Chambersburg PA
CBHW030944210726
48290CB00007B/2324